MORGAN'S MERCENARIES
IV
MAVERICK HEARTS

She was beautiful.

Without thinking, Jake rose to his feet. It was part of his officer's training to stand in the presence of women, despite his feeling that no woman was up to the job that lay ahead of him.

"Are you…" he began awkwardly, holding out his hand toward her. Somehow, he wished she wasn't his team partner. She was too beautiful, too feminine looking to be qualified for such a risky venture.

Ana smiled shyly. "Jake Travers?" His gaze assessed her as if she were stripped naked before him. Girding herself, she tried to cooly return his arrogant gaze.

Jake felt his skin tighten at the sound of his name on her lips. He managed a curt nod. "Yeah, I'm Jake Travers." He sounded as snarly as he felt.

"Well," she asked lightly, "do I meet with your approval?"

Jake scowled. "That remains to be seen…."

Dear Reader,

What if…? These two little words serve as the springboard for each romance novel that bestselling author Joan Elliott Pickart writes. "I always go back to that age-old question. My ideas come straight from imagination," she says. And with more than thirty Silhouette novels to her credit, the depth of Joan's imagination seems bottomless! Joan started by taking a class to learn how to write a romance and "felt that this was where I belonged," she recalls. This month Joan delivers *Her Little Secret,* the next from THE BABY BET, where you'll discover what if…a sheriff and a lovely nursery owner decide to foil town matchmakers and "act" like lovers.…

And don't miss the other compelling "what ifs" in this month's Silhouette Special Edition lineup. What if a U.S. Marshal knee-deep in his father's murder investigation discovers his former love is expecting his child? Read *Seven Months and Counting…* by Myrna Temte, the next installment in the STOCKWELLS OF TEXAS series. What if an army ranger, who believes dangerous missions are no place for a woman, learns the only person who can help rescue his sister is a female? Lindsay McKenna brings you this exciting story in *Man with a Mission,* the next book in her MORGAN'S MERCENARIES: MAVERICK HEARTS series. What happens if a dutiful daughter falls in love with the one man her family forbids? Look for Christine Flynn's *Forbidden Love.* What if a single dad falls for a pampered beauty who is not at all accustomed to small-town happily-ever-after? Find out in Nora Roberts's *Considering Kate,* the next in THE STANISLASKIS. And what if the girl-next-door transforms herself to get a man's attention—but is noticed by someone else? Make sure to pick up Barbara McMahon's *Starting with a Kiss.*

What if… Two words with endless possibilities. If you've got your own "what if" scenario, start writing. Silhouette Special Edition would love to read about it.

Happy reading!

Karen Taylor Richman,
Senior Editor

Please address questions and book requests to:
Silhouette Reader Service
U.S.: 3010 Walden Ave., P.O. Box 1325, Buffalo, NY 14269
Canadian: P.O. Box 609, Fort Erie, Ont. L2A 5X3

Man with a Mission

LINDSAY McKENNA

SPECIAL EDITION™

Published by Silhouette Books

America's Publisher of Contemporary Romance

To my editor, Lynda Curnyn. Thank you for all your
help, your support and belief in my plots and characters.

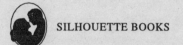 SILHOUETTE BOOKS

ISBN 0-373-24376-6

MAN WITH A MISSION

Copyright © 2001 by Lindsay McKenna

This edition published by arrangement with Harlequin Books S.A.

® and TM are trademarks of Harlequin Books S.A., used under license.
Trademarks indicated with ® are registered in the United States Patent
and Trademark Office, the Canadian Trade Marks Office and in other
countries.

Visit Silhouette at www.eHarlequin.com

Printed in U.S.A.

Books by Lindsay McKenna

LINDSAY McKENNA

is a practicing homeopath and emergency medical technician on the Navajo Reservation. She lives with her husband, David, near Sedona.

THIS MONTH
you'll find bold adventure and passionate romance
in Silhouette Special Edition
as

Lindsay McKenna

continues her popular series,
MORGAN'S MERCENARIES: MAVERICK HEARTS

Morgan's men are born for battle—
but are they ready for love?

NEXT MONTH
look for Captain Maya Stevenson's story in
an all-new, longer-length single title book:
MORGAN'S MERCENARIES: HEART OF STONE

Available from Silhouette Books
at your favorite retail outlets!

Chapter One

"Hey! You can't go in there, Captain Travers!"

Morgan raised his head at the sound of his assistant's voice. He was in conference with Mike Houston and Pilar Martinez, both of whom had flown in from Peru, and was going over some February reports with them when the door to his office was pushed open. A tall, scowling, dark-haired man, around age thirty, strode into the war room, with tiny, blond-haired Jenny Wright tugging on his right arm in a futile attempt to stop his progress. Morgan's assistant looked like a gnat attacking a massive Cape buffalo.

Mike Houston automatically rose, unsure who the man who had crashed their conference was. He went on guard, his hand moving to the holstered pistol he wore beneath his dark blue blazer.

Morgan sat back, his gaze sweeping the stranger's tense, hard features. The look of desperation and apology in his assistant's wide blue eyes told him everything. Holding up his hand, he murmured, "It's all right, Jenny. Let him go."

Jenny released the stranger's arm. She was breathing hard. Diminutive compared to his bulk and height, she glared up at him, her hands set petulantly on her hips. "I'm really sorry, Morgan. I *tried* to stop him. He wouldn't take no for an answer. I'm really sorry...." She brushed several strands of gold hair from her gathered brows.

Morgan turned his narrowed eyes upon the young stranger, who was dressed in camel-colored slacks, a matching blazer and a white shirt open at the collar. There was casual elegance to the man's attire, but Morgan detected an obvious military bearing in the way he squared his shoulders and stood, feet slightly apart, hands at his sides, as if waiting for a counterattack.

"And you are?" Morgan asked in a deep tone.

"My name is Captain Jake Travers, Mr. Trayhern." He turned to Morgan's assistant. There was apology in his low, strained voice. "I'm sorry, Ms. Wright. I *have* to see Mr. Trayhern. I didn't mean to upset you."

Jenny scowled up at him, her jaw set, her full lips thinned. "The world wants to see Mr. Trayhern! What makes you think *you* are better than anyone else and can just bust in here like this? The nerve!"

Morgan squelched a smile. Jenny, the young woman he had hired when his old assistant retired a year earlier, was only five foot two and barely a hundred pounds soaking wet, but she was fiercely protective. Like a willful, loyal terrier, once she latched on to something with her teeth, she didn't let go. The tiny dynamo had dreams of being a mercenary someday. Morgan hated to break the news to her that she'd never be one. Jenny had no military or police background. But she had a wonderful, romantic side to her, and Morgan sensed that in her dream of dreams, she'd like to be a heroine like the women he already had in his employ at Perseus. Jenny idolized all the mercenaries. She loved working at Perseus, and if the truth be known, she was the best assistant he'd ever had. "It's all right, Jenny. Why don't you bring us some coffee? Mr. Travers here looks like he could use a cup."

Jake nodded hesitantly. "Yes, sir, I could use some coffee about now...." He gave Jenny another apologetic glance. "I'm very sorry, Ms. Wright... I hope you can forgive me?"

Jenny looked at Morgan. "Okay," she muttered with defiance, "I'll get the coffee." She jerked her tiny chin up at Jake. "And no, I don't forgive you!" Then she turned on her heel and stalked out, shutting the door firmly behind her.

Morgan felt Mike move from his tense position, though he never took his eyes off Jake Travers. Pilar, who was on his right, was studying the intruder intently, too.

"Well, Captain Travers, now that you have our full, undivided attention, would you like to come and sit down over here," Morgan said, pointing to a chair near where they were sitting, "and tell us what's so important that you breached all my security to get here?" There was amusement in his tone.

"I'm no longer a captain, sir." Jake stood watching the wary-looking man to the left of Morgan Trayhern. He knew him. He was Major Mike Houston, a legendary figure in the U.S. Army, a special forces officer who had made a big difference in Peru by chasing down and stopping the drug cartels in that country.

"Oh?" Morgan said mildly.

Jake opened his hand. "I resigned my commission yesterday, sir. The army wouldn't let me go after my sister, who has been kidnapped by a drug lord in Peru. I told them to go to hell. I'll move heaven and earth to find her…and I need your help…."

"Whoa, slow down, Son," Morgan said. "Come on, sit down. Let's talk this out."

Mike relaxed once he realized Jake Travers was an officer in the U.S. Army, just as Mike himself had been at one time. A lot of people had a price on Morgan's life, which was why the head of Perseus kept his main office hidden deep in the Rocky Mountains of Montana. No one, except for this petulant upstart of an army officer, had ever found Morgan, or been able to get through all the tight security set up for Perseus employees who worked at the Philipsburg office. Until now. That said something about Jake Travers's cunning and abilities. He deserved time with Morgan based upon his daring.

"Yes, sir." Jake gave Mike and the woman a penitent glance as he moved toward the long, oval table and the chairs surrounding it. "I apologize for my lack of manners and appointment."

Chuckling, Morgan gave Houston a bemused look as Jake sat down. Jenny entered with a tray bearing white china cups, a coffee dispenser, cream, sugar, and cinnamon rolls for the four of them. She set it down near Travers. Giving him a dark look of disapproval, she quickly poured everyone coffee, then left.

Morgan reached for one of the small cinnamon rolls, which were baked on the premises every morning for himself and his employees. When he saw Travers giving them a longing look, he said, "Have some, Captain? You appear a little hungry around the edges."

Jake didn't hesitate. He was starving. "Thank you, sir. And, as I mentioned earlier, you can dispense with my title. I'm no longer in the army... I'm a civilian now."

Houston folded his hands and watched the young officer. "You're a ranger, aren't you?"

Jake looked up, startled. "Is it written all over me, despite my civilian clothes, sir?"

Houston smiled a little. "It takes one to know one. Your stance. The way you carry yourself. Your alertness."

Jake gobbled down three of the small cinnamon rolls, then sheepishly drank most of his coffee and poured himself more.

"I think Señor Travers needed this breakfast," Pilar noted, smiling gently. "How long has it been since you've last eaten?"

Jake felt heat moving up his neck and into his face. The three of them were studying him with kindly looks; they weren't laughing at him. Sitting back, the delicate white cup decorated with purple and yellow violets looking tiny in his massive hands, he muttered, "About twelve hours, ma'am. I left Fort Benning, Georgia, and have been patching together transportation across the U.S. to get here."

"You were with the 75th Ranger Regiment?" Mike asked mildly.

"Yes, sir, I was." He sipped the hot coffee with relish, his gaze darting from one to the other. Jake had no idea how he would be received. Morgan Trayhern, the man he had to see, seemed slightly entertained by his impromptu entrance. Houston was more assessing. And the beautiful black-haired woman, whose cultured voice had a distinct Spanish accent, had a look of compassion in her sparkling eyes. Still, his stomach was knotted and tense.

Mike nodded. "Good outfit. So why'd they let you resign your commission to come out here and see us?"

"Sir, it's about my sister, Talia Travers." Jake sat up, his back rigid with stress. Setting the cup aside, he said in an emotional, strained voice, "You've got to help me find her. Please…"

"Slow down, Son," Morgan murmured, wiping his hands on a linen napkin. "Start from the beginning, will you?"

Chastened, Jake nodded. "My sister, Talia—Tal— is two years younger than me. She's a hydrologist. She looks for water and tells people where to dig a well, basically. She's one of the best and brightest out of Ohio State University. She's always wanted to help the poor and the underprivileged. Last year she quit a very high-paying job with a U.S. firm and took a position for one-quarter of the money, with the Wiraqocha Foundation.''

Mike's brows rose. "I know of them."

Morgan glanced at him. "Oh?"

"Yeah," Mike murmured. "They're a legit nonprofit organization out of California that works with the Que'ro Indians, the last of the Inkan bloodlines, up in the mountains of Peru. Last I heard, they were sinking water wells up in the Rainbow Valley area, which is about a hundred miles northwest of Cusco, near the gateway to Machu Picchu Reserve."

Relief flooded Jake. "Yes, sir, that's them. That's who my sister went to work for. She just went down there on her first assignment, to find six places to sink wells, at different Que'ro villages in that region." He was so glad someone knew the area.

"Go on," Morgan murmured.

"Tal went down there two weeks ago. We spoke just before she left from Dallas–Fort Worth International Airport to hop a flight down to Lima. She was really excited. She was to head up a team of hydrologists and other water experts from Peru, who were going to meet her in Cusco and make plans to put in the new wells. You see, sir, sixty percent of the children in those villages die because of bad water." Jake shook his head and frowned. "Sixty percent, sir. Well, Tal has a big, soft heart, and when she found out little babies and young children were dying at those rates, she went to the Wiraqocha Foundation and offered her services to try and turn those numbers around. I mean—'' he opened his hand helplessly ''—if it was your child that died because of bad water...''

Morgan nodded. ''I understand,'' he said softly. ''Your sister is to be commended for her courage in helping those people.''

''Yes, sir.'' Jake swallowed hard. ''The Wiraqocha Foundation just contacted me to tell me my sister had gone missing and they suspect kidnapping. The last time I heard from Tal was last week. She called from Cusco to say she was going out in the field, near what she called the Inka Trail. There's a village located nearby, and that's where I believe she was when she was kidnapped.''

''The Inka Trail,'' Mike told Morgan, ''is an ancient route about a hundred miles long that connects the Rainbow Valley to the temple site at Machu Picchu. It's about a thousand years old, paved with stones that were laid by the Inkan people so that runners from the empire's main temple at Cusco could send messages to different sites in the valley, all the way to Machu Picchu.''

''And today,'' Pilar added, ''it's considered one of the most beautiful and challenging trails in the world. People from around the world walk it just to say they did it and survived.'' She smiled a little. ''The trail goes from fourteen thousand feet down to six thousand. And it's not for wimps.''

Houston chuckled. ''No joke.'' Then he became somber. ''That area you're talking about has never had drug activity—until now. Did your sister know of any activity before she went down there?''

Shaking his head, Jake muttered, ''No, sir. She didn't say anything about it, and frankly, I didn't think about it, either. This foundation has been working in Peru for over a decade and never heard of drugs being traded through Rainbow Valley. They are just as shocked and upset over Tal's disappearance as my parents and I are.''

Houston nodded. ''Drug lords move around. They never stay in one spot too long. They keep alive by remaining on the move.'' He got up and went to a wall map of Peru, which had a number of small red flags pinned to it. He picked up the flag near the Rainbow Valley region. ''Just as I thought,'' he muttered, reading the tag, ''the last report of drug activity we received from this area implicates a small-time drug lord who's trying to enlarge his territory.'' Mike pinned the flag back on the map and came over and sat down.

''By any chance is it Javier Rojas?'' Pilar asked, looking up at Mike.

''Yep, that'd be my bet,'' he answered. ''A mean little snake with tiny, close-set eyes and a personality to match. He's well known for kidnapping foreigners and then demanding money for them. It's how he does business, getting more money to set up his little drug-smuggling kingdom.''

Jake scowled. ''There's been no word from anyone on Tal's disappearance. The Wiraqocha Foundation has received no demands for money for her release, either. And neither have my parents. Is that bad?''

Morgan heard the carefully concealed terror in the young officer's voice. He saw it in his pale blue eyes, in his huge black pupils. Jake leaned forward, his hands balled into fists on the table, the desperation and worry for his sister obvious.

"Look, Son, I think Pilar and Mike will agree with me that when you're dealing with a small fish like Rojas, a phone call or demand for money at this point may be a bit premature." Morgan looked to his people. "Am I correct?"

"That's right," Pilar said. She reached across the table and patted Jake's hand gently. "You must remember, *señor,* that Peru is not like *Norteamérica.* In Peru we do not have superior roads."

"No roads at all, most of the time," Mike added wryly. "A lot of llama, alpaca and cow trails, though."

"*Sí.* And telephones are a luxury. Especially anywhere outside of Lima, the capital, or Cusco, the second largest city in our country."

"Translated," Houston growled, "that means that Rojas doesn't have an iridium satellite phone, which he could use to call anywhere in the world, because he can't yet afford one. He can't use a cell phone up there in those mountains, either. So he's got to get back to Cusco, would be my guess, to get to a phone to make a call. Which—" Mike smiled a little "—can be difficult at best. If he's the struggling little upstart of a drug lord I think he is, he doesn't have the money, the means or the people to do this. It's probably too soon to expect a call."

"But what about Tal? What will he do to her?"

Jake choked back the emotion rising in his chest and jamming his throat. He wanted to cry. He wanted to scream. He wanted to wrap his fingers around Rojas's scrawny little neck and choke him to death if he was the one who had kidnapped Tal. What would the man do to her? Rape her? Bitterness coated Jake's mouth. Jake couldn't stand the thought of such a thing happening to his vibrant sister, who was like sunshine in his life.

Houston sighed. "What kind of a personality does Tal have?"

"She's outgoing. Spirited. Vibrant. She walks into a room and everyone turns to look at her." Jake smiled a little, his voice softening. "She's such a warm person, Major Houston. Very caring."

"Is she a pushover?" Pilar asked.

Jake shook his head. "No, just the opposite. She's a fighter. She can confront the meanest bastard and look him in the eye and stand toe-to-toe with him and win."

Houston nodded approvingly. "Good. Because mealymouthed tyrants like Rojas are usually afraid of big, bruising *norteamericana* women, who are seen as Amazon warriors. South American men are used to passive females who do their bidding." He glanced past Morgan and gave Pilar an apologetic look. "There *are* exceptions, of course."

Pilar nodded deferentially. "Thank you, Mike."

Jake looked at them. "You're saying that if she stays strong, he won't…hurt her?"

"That's right," Houston murmured. "She probably scares the pants off Rojas." He chuckled.

Pilar laughed softly. "South American men have not learned how to deal with a strong, self-empowered woman yet." Her dark eyes sparkled mischievously. "But they are learning."

Jake leaned forward. "That leads me to why I'm here, Mr. Trayhern. I need to get down there. I need help, though. The kind only you can give me. Can you send me with one of your mercenaries as a guide? So I can find Tal? My parents are Iowa farmers. They don't have any money at all, but I've got about ten thousand dollars saved and—"

"Save your money," Morgan murmured. He looked at Mike. "Who do we have in from a mission that we could send down with him?"

Mike rolled his eyes. "No one. We're stretched thin right now, Morgan."

Scowling, he said, "Are you sure?"

Mike nodded glumly. "Very sure."

Pilar sat up. "Then you need someone from inside Peru to assist you. Mike, what about Captain Maya Stevenson? She's got a spec ops—special operations—base near Machu Picchu, right?"

Snapping his fingers, Houston sat up. "That's right! She's got Apache helicopter pilots from various countries working under her command. And if I recall, there are two Peruvian pilots among them. Home grown. The kind we need right now."

Pilar grinned a little. "What are the chances of persuading Captain Stevenson to loan out a pilot who might know not only the area, but the Quechua language as well? The Rainbow Valley is mostly made up of Quechua Indian villages, where Spanish is a second language, not the first, as it is in the rest of the country.''

Morgan looked from Mike to Pilar. ''Sounds good to me. What you don't know is that I've been in contact with her already. I got wind, through an army general friend of mine, of her needing upgraded Apache helicopters. She indicated that she might be willing to work with us in order to get those upgrades. I haven't told her how we might work with her.''

Jake frowned. ''I don't understand. You don't have a team or a person from Perseus who can help me find Tal?''

''No, Son, we don't.'' Morgan smiled slightly. ''But we have other contacts that might work out just as well. Maybe better. Mike, you want to contact Captain Stevenson on the iridium scramble sat com? Tell her I want to trade one of her Peruvian women pilots for those Apache upgrades she's been wanting.'' He scowled. ''She won't be easily convinced, Mike, so hang tough with her. She's shorthanded as hell and isn't about to let one go unless we wave those much-needed upgrades under her nose. She's a savvy negotiator.''

Rising, Mike said, ''You bet. Hang around, Captain Travers, and I'll be back in a few minutes.''

Nonplussed, Jake looked at Morgan. ''Who's this Captain Stevenson?''

''She's a shadowy spec ops figure who is under spook supervision. We don't know a whole lot about her, as her work is on a need-to-know basis. The general I talked to put me in touch with her about a month ago.''

Spooks were the CIA, Jake realized. "A woman helicopter pilot down in Peru and working for the CIA?"

"Actually," Pilar added proudly, "she's a U.S. Army captain, an Apache combat helicopter pilot. One of yours. How about that?"

"She's army?"

Morgan looked amused. "Why does that surprise you, Captain Travers? Women make just as lethal warriors as any man ever did. In fact—" he smiled over at Pilar "—my women mercenaries, most of whom are from one of the four military services, are equal to or better than any man in my employ. There're no weak sisters among them. And I like teaming up a man *with* a woman because women see things men often overlook. And in our business, the devil's in the details. You overlook a detail and you're dead. So, yes, my women are like big guard dogs, with senses far better honed than any man's probably ever will be. Men and women each have their strong points. Together, they've got the best chance of carrying out a mission successfully and coming home alive."

"You've made quite a few sexist statements there, Morgan. And for a change, most of them favor women," Pilar said, her grin widening, pride in her eyes.

Morgan shrugged. "I've learned it the hard way over the years, Pilar. Never underestimate a woman who's doing spy duties. She sees all the colors and has finely honed instincts." He grinned at her. "You were a spy down in Peru for quite some time."

Pilar nodded. "Yes, I was. And I was very good at what I did."

"Men have just as good an ability to see details as any woman, sir," Jake said.

Morgan studied him across the table. Jake was scowling now, as if he didn't want to hear that a woman was as good—or better—than any man.

"Captain, I dare say you're young and inexperienced. If you were a ranger, you have no women in your outfit—yet. And that's a pity, in my opinion, because they bring skills and abilities to the table none of us males have ever gotten in touch with. They can teach you a lot if you're open to learning from them."

Jake throttled his defensive response. "Beggin' your pardon, sir, but no woman can do the job a ranger does. Ever."

Pilar sighed. "Oh, Captain, you are so young and wet behind the ears."

Chuckling, Morgan said, "If you don't value what a woman brings to the table, Son, then it's your loss. Captain Stevenson has single-handedly carved out a spec ops in the Peruvian jungle in the last three years, with a small group of women U.S. Army pilots and women technicians to service the crafts. She's cut drug running from Peru to Bolivia's border by fifty percent. Just she and her women. Major Houston was down there for ten years trying to do the same thing, but he didn't have near the success rate she's had. Captain Stevenson is a bold, brilliant woman. A strong tactical planner and a visionary way ahead of her time."

"She's also a pit bull when it comes to drug runners," Pilar added grimly. Studying Travers, she said, "Captain Stevenson is a legend in her own time down there. She's feared by every drug lord in Peru. Her Boeing Apache combat choppers confront Russian Kamov Black Shark helicopters daily in the skies over Peru, stopping the cocaine from being taken over the border to Bolivia. She and her pilots are the bravest we know."

Houston reentered the room, a big smile on his features. "Good news, Morgan. I got Captain Stevenson on the iridium sat phone." He came over and sat down, holding a piece of paper covered with scribbled handwriting.

Looking at Travers, he said, "You're in luck. Captain Stevenson has one Peruvian pilot who was born in the Rainbow Valley—Lieutenant Ana Lucia Cortina, twenty-seven years old. Her mother was a Que'ro Indian, her father an art gallery owner from Lima. Ana knows the Rainbow Valley region and the Inka Trail like the back of her hand."

"Is Captain Stevenson willing to loan Ana to us for this mission to find Jake's sister?" Morgan asked.

"Yeah...for the price you mentioned. You know, they're shorthanded as hell down there. Maya only has twelve pilots. They fly three pilots a day, in the two Apaches and an old, antique Cobra. It's a twenty-four-hour tour. The pilots then go to standby status for another twenty-four hours, and then the third day they get off, to rest. Actually, they're not resting at all right now because she's shorthanded in personnel, too, so they're doing a lot of collateral duty."

Mike sighed and tapped his finger on the paper. "That means that if Captain Stevenson releases Ana to us, to help Jake and be his guide, than she's *really* going to be shorthanded. Her other pilots must take up the slack while Ana is gone."

"So, the Apache upgrade will compensate her for this?" Morgan demanded.

Houston grinned. "Yes, sir, it will."

"Fine. That's not a problem. How about long-term?"

"She's hurting for money *and* people, plus that upgrade. She needs updated, more modern Apaches, which you're going to provide. They're flying the old A model, the first of their type. They've got the new Longbows out, which are incredible, and before you stepped into the picture, she couldn't afford them, either. What she needs is an IV transfusion of money, the new D model upgrade *and* people down there to sustain her in her efforts."

"We'll look into this further," Morgan assured him. "I'm very interested in her setup down there and think we can work together. Maybe we can lend her a hand in a lot of different ways. We'll just have to see...."

Houston nodded. He looked across the table at Travers. "They're sending a faxed photo of Lieutenant Cortina to us in the next hour, plus some background info on her. Captain Stevenson says you're to meet Lieutenant Cortina in Agua Caliente, Peru. That's a little backwater town at the base of Machu Picchu.

"Captain Stevenson uses the local civilian helicopter that flies in and out of there to ferry her people discreetly from their base, hidden deep in the jungle, to and from this civilian town. Agua Caliente is their formal link with civilization and Cusco, which is the major city they work out of when necessary. Captain Stevenson said Lieutenant Cortina will pose as a *tourista,* which is normally how her people infiltrate from the military to civilian status. You're to meet her at—'' he looked at the name closely ''—a French restaurant named India Feliz—Happy Indian—just off the main plaza. At 1100 hours two days from now.'' Mike looked up. ''You got your passport in order?''

Jake swallowed hard. ''Yes, sir, I do...but...a *woman?* Sir, if this is as dangerous as it sounds, I really don't want a woman tagging along with me.''

Mike gave Morgan a pointed look.

''Captain Travers,'' Morgan growled, ''I don't think you heard a word we just said. Women are as good as, if not better than, any male out there in the world of spy and stealth combat. I'm sure this Lieutenant Cortina is not going to be a noose around your neck. It will probably be the other way around.'' He allowed a slight, one-cornered grin to appear on his mouth.

Stunned, Jake stared at the two men. He saw Pilar sitting back, frowning. He knew he'd insulted her. ''But—''

''No buts,'' Morgan said. ''You want your sister back, Captain?''

''Well...yes, sir, I do, but—''

''Dammit, man,'' Mike said, irritated, ''don't throw up this macho *mano a mano* stuff with us. It doesn't fly. Our women are equal to our men. Period. Captain Stevenson said your best bet is to use Lieutenant Cortina. She knows the valley. She was *born* there. She speaks five languages fluently. You speak any but English?''

Stung, Jake growled, ''I speak Spanish.''

Mike shrugged. ''Then you aren't going to be as bad a liability as I first thought. Just know that Spanish is a *second* language down in the valley, Captain. Quechua is first, and Lieutenant Cortina speaks it fluently because she *is* part Quechuan. Got it?''

''Yes, sir, I got it.''

Morgan tapped his fingers briskly on the table and studied Travers from beneath his dark eyebrows. ''I hear the words of agreement from you, Captain, but I sure as hell hear something else in your voice that says you want to take over this mission and do what you think is best. Well, that's *not* going to happen. Lieutenant Cortina is in charge of this mission. You got that?''

Jake's mouth fell open. ''That's impossible, sir!''

''Sit down, Captain. There's more,'' Morgan snarled.

Jake sat down rigidly, breathing hard. A woman! And on top of it all, as *his* commander? *Not a chance!*

Jabbing his finger at the ranger, Morgan said, ''Lieutenant Cortina *runs* this mission. If she tells you to jump, you ask how high. Got it?''

''I don't feel, sir, that any woman can successfully undertake such a mission.''

Morgan gave him a frustrated glare. ''Then you do

not want our help, Captain Travers. Go find your sister on your own.''

Gulping unsteadily, Jake looked at Morgan's set face, his glacial blue eyes burning holes through him. The man meant what he said and Jake knew it. Morgan Trayhern was not bluffing. Sitting there, Jake chewed over his options. He desperately needed someone who knew the Rainbow Valley region. He needed an interpreter. Smarting beneath their collective glares, Jake looked down at his hands, which were clenched in his lap beneath the table. Grief and worry over Tal warred with his belief that a woman could never do a man's job, especially a job like this one. What were his options?

If he flew to Peru on his own, he'd have to hire a guide and interpreter. Could the guide be trusted? How could Jake know for *sure* he'd find someone who wasn't a drug runner, working for the drug lord of the valley? The only thing Jake had going for him was his knowledge of Spanish. That and his skills as a ranger, which would definitely be an asset in this situation.

Still…Tal's life was hanging in the balance. Could he let his personal beliefs and male pride keep him from coming to her rescue? She could die because he refused to work with a woman. A shudder ran through him. He compressed his lips and raised his head.

''All right,'' Jake rasped unsteadily, ''I'll work with Lieutenant Cortina.''

Morgan's glare cut through him. ''I want to hear you promise me that you'll be her *subordinate* in this, Captain Travers. That you'll accept her leadership, her authority and her status as commander on this mission.''

Swallowing hard, Jake muttered, "I accept Lieutenant Cortina as my commander on this spec ops."

There was a long, strained silence in the room after he spoke. Jake looked anxiously at Morgan, and then at the thin-lipped, scowling Mike Houston. Both men traded glances. Mike spoke first.

"You realize, Captain Travers, that if you're just mouthing words on this, we'll be following your mission down there and will know at once? We refuse to jeopardize Lieutenant Cortina's life if you decide to get up on your male testosterone motorcycle and try to take over. She'll be carrying an iridium satellite phone on her person at all times. Captain Stevenson, as we speak, is giving Lieutenant Cortina the mission profile that I had faxed down to her earlier.

"Lieutenant Cortina will know that she's the commander on this little adventure," Mike continued. "She's your best chance to find your sister and get her out alive. You aren't. You're a gringo, a foreigner, while Ana Cortina knows Peru by heart. The sooner you let go of your damned male pride and surrender to her knowledge of the terrain, the people and the environment, the sooner your sister will be found, hopefully alive and unharmed. But the more you try to siphon off her authority or command, the more the chances of your sister being found at all, much less alive, deteriorate rapidly. Do you understand that?" Mike's gaze nailed him directly.

Flexing his fists beneath the table, Jake muttered, "Yes, sir, I got it."

Morgan sighed. "I don't know that I feel you're trustworthy on this matter, Captain Travers. However, for the sake of your sister, who's the innocent in all of this, I'm going to approve this mission. The moment I hear, or Mike Houston hears, of you sabotaging Lieutenant Cortina in any way, I'll have your ass pulled out of Peru so fast it will make even your seasoned military head spin. Do we understand one another? And if that happens, then you can consider your sister *dead*. All the choices and decisions are *yours*, Captain Travers. Work as a team or else."

Holding his anger in check, Jake nodded. "I hear you, sir. And I'm grateful for your help. Tal's the important one here, not me. Not what I believe."

"Fine," Morgan said crisply, standing. He buttoned his dark gray coat. "Let's go out and look at the photo and file that I'm sure have come in by now."

Jake rose. He felt relief, though he was still angry. More than anything, he bridled silently over the fact that he was going to have a woman as his commanding officer on this mission. Of all the hurdles and trials he knew were before him as he tried to locate Tal, he'd never figured that a woman would also be thrown into this murky, dangerous situation. *Dammit.*

Chapter Two

A soft knock on Maya Stevenson's door made her lift her head from the slew of paperwork that littered her desk. Her door was always open, but her people gave a perfunctory knock anyway.

"Come in, Ana." She gestured to the wooden chair to the left of her desk. "Have a seat." She noticed that Lieutenant Ana Lucia Cortina was in her black, snug-fitting helicopter uniform, her helmet tucked beneath her left arm. She had been on twenty-four-hour duty and had just flown a mission four hours ago. She looked tired. There were smudges beneath her glorious cinnamon-colored eyes. Her ebony hair, frayed from wearing the helmet, was still in a chignon at the nape of her slender neck.

"Hi…thanks…" Ana gave Maya a slight, weary smile.

"How'd the flight go?" Maya noticed as Ana set the helmet down on the desk that she looked drawn. Maya knew why. The death of her fiancé a year ago was still wearing on Ana. And Maya knew that today was Roberto's birthday. He would have been twenty-eight years old, if he'd lived. She wished that she could love someone as much as Ana had loved Roberto, but no man had entered her life to make her feel that way. Maya had long ago given up hoping such a man existed for her.

"We got jumped by a Kamov Black Shark helicopter flown by Faro Valentino's Russian mercenaries near the Bolivian border," Ana murmured, sitting down in the chair. Lifting her long, slender arms, she pulled her black hair out of the tight knot at the base of her neck, shook her head and allowed the strands to tumble across her proud shoulders. "Nothing new. I took a few bullet holes in the fuselage of my Apache, but otherwise, no casualties. My crew is going to have to check it to make sure no bullets have nicked the cables in that area, but that's all."

"Hmm." Maya frowned, tinkering with the silver pen between her fingers. "Get any rockets off at them?"

One corner of Ana's full mouth lifted slightly. "Oh, yes. We got close but didn't bring it down." She scowled, her fine, thin black brows bunching. "I just wish we had radar capability to pick up their signature, Maya. Whatever kind of paint they've got on those Kamovs, we can't detect them, and they jump us from behind every time. One of these days we're going to get shot down," she said, grimacing.

"I know…what we need are those new Boeing D model Apaches that came out last year. I hear through the transom that they still don't pick up the Black Shark signature, but at least we'd have a better helo than our Russian counterpart in every other way. Right now, we're hurting. Our budget can't afford one."

Ana ran her fingers through her hair and massaged her scalp. "Ugh, that helmet is so heavy. I get a headache every time." She opened her eyes and smiled at Maya, who was dressed in the same type of black uniform. Her commanding officer's black hair was a little longer than hers, and she wore it down when she didn't have to fly. "I've given up hope of us ever getting the new D model, Maya. The U.S. Army wants to ignore the fact that we're down here doing a fine job of stopping drug runners from reaching the Bolivian border. Because we're a bunch of upstart women army officers."

"Humph, isn't *that* the truth." Maya set the pen aside and leaned back in her creaky old leather chair. Outside her opened door, women clerks who worked in the headquarters building of their base, hidden deep inside a cave, moved up and down the corridor like worker bees. Keeping her voice down, Maya said to Ana, "I have a project for you, if you want it."

Perking up, Ana said, "Oh? What? Do I get some R and R over in Agua Caliente? Do I get to stay in Gringo Bill's Hostel and rest up? I'm *dying* for one of Patrick's mocha lattes at India Feliz Restaurant." She laughed softly, knowing that they were far too shorthanded for Maya to give her a well deserved day off.

Maya picked up a fax, rose and stretched across her desk to hand it to Ana. "No, sorry. I know you deserve some downtime. How'd you like to work with this guy? He's a former U.S. Army Ranger captain."

Ana took the flimsy piece of paper. The black-and-white photo of a man, his face square, eyes penetrating, mouth full but unsmiling, stared back at her. For whatever reason, Ana's heart gave a lurch. Puzzled as to why, she studied the photo, which showed the army officer in his military uniform, ribbons and all. She recognized the parachute wings on the left breast pocket, and the ribbons he'd accrued were impressive. Despite his rock-hard expression, Ana's intuition told her this was a man with a heart and a conscience. She had nothing to prove that, of course; it was simply something she felt to be true. And in her business as a combat pilot, her intuition was more finely honed than most. She relied on it heavily, and it had never been wrong yet.

Puzzled over why her heart had lurched unexpectedly, Ana remembered that today was Roberto's birthday. The day that they had set for their wedding. Grief flowed through her momentarily. Well, that would never be, now. Roberto had been killed while aboard his Peruvian Navy cruiser, shot by drug runners. That was a year ago. Rubbing her heart, Ana looked up. She saw Maya studying her intently. Ana knew that look and smiled slightly.

"Okay, boss, what's up? You're sitting there looking at me like a jaguar eyeing a good meal.'' Ana raised the fax and waved it a little. ''He's not an Apache pilot. He's a ground pounder.''

Grinning, Maya said, ''Yeah, he's not one of us. He's in the doggy corps.''

They both laughed. There was infamous rivalry between the U.S. Army aviation corps and the rest of the troops, which handled ground duty.

''I've just been told there's a special assignment and we've been tapped for it,'' Maya told her. ''This man's sister, Talia Travers, is a hydrologist. She finds water so wells can be dug. Anyway, she was over in Rainbow Valley when she suddenly disappeared. The foundation she works for called Jake Travers, the guy in the photo. When he tried to get the army to give him TDY—temporary duty—so he could come down here and search for his sister, they refused. So he resigned.''

''Wow,'' Ana murmured, ''that's a pretty rash and reckless thing to do with your career, but I don't blame him under the circumstances. Family is more important.''

''Yeah, isn't it though?'' Maya shook her head. ''Typical out-of-step army higher-ups made the wrong decision—again. They just lost a good man and an officer. Anyway…Travers went to a spook ops organization known as Perseus. I have a friend who works with them—Mike Houston. He contacted me about this mission. What they need is a guide, Ana, to help Travers locate his sister. You're the obvious choice. You were born at Ollytatambu at the neck of the Rainbow Valley. No one knows that huge valley like you do. You grew up climbing the mountains and walking the hundred-mile-long Inka Trail that winds through it.'' Maya smiled briefly. ''So I thought you might like to take this TDY. How about it?''

Frowning, Ana studied the officer's stony countenance once more. ''What do they suspect? Druggies? A kidnapping?''

''Yeah, but no one's called in a kidnap demand to Travers's parents or to anyone else. Houston suspects it's Rojas, a small-time, local drug lord trying to position himself higher up on that ladder by moving into Rainbow Valley and grabbing a rich *norteamericana*, like Tal Travers. She's not rich, but he doesn't know that—yet. Rojas is obviously not so wealthy as to have an iridium sat phone on him. They cost four thousand dollars U.S. And even regular phones aren't common in Rainbow Valley. My hunch is he's holding on to her until he can get to Cusco to make the call.''

''Mmm.'' Ana looked around the office. ''Do you have the latest list of drug runners from my old stomping grounds?''

Grinning a little, Maya handed her a short list of names. ''Yeah, here they are.''

Studying them, Ana shrugged. ''Could be any one of them. But they mentioned Rojas as a possibility?''

''Yes. You know any of them from your days growing up there?''

Tapping the paper, Ana murmured, ''Just one— Rojas. I remember him at school. As I recall, he was a slum kid from the poor side of Lima whose parents dumped him in the Rainbow Valley to get rid of him because he was embarrassing the family by stealing stuff down there. I didn't know him personally. I had a tutor who came to our villa every day to teach me. I only heard about him. He was a real bully, I guess.''

"Knowing what you know now," Maya murmured, "do you want the assignment? I anticipate it will take a week or less to locate Tal Travers, one way or another."

"Gosh, Maya…what will you do without me on the pilot roster? That's going to leave you short-handed as heck. Only eleven pilots to fly the missions.''

"I'll take your flight duty and missions while you're gone. Don't worry about it." How like Ana to be concerned about everyone else first. That was one more thing Maya liked about her close-knit, all-female team who worked at this hidden base fifty miles from Machu Picchu, the huge tourist attraction in Peru.

Rubbing her wrinkled, broad brow, Ana said, "Well…sure, I'd love to do this. A little change of pace. I don't get home often enough anymore, so I'll really enjoy getting back to my old haunts." She felt her tiredness leave at the thought of getting a break from the brutal flying duty.

"Excellent," Maya said. "Then it's settled. You're to meet this dude at Agua Caliente, at our normal meeting place—India Feliz Restaurant. Patrick, the owner and chef there, will set up the meeting on the second floor so that you two have optimum, uninterrupted time to talk and plan this mission." She looked at her watch. "Captain Travers will be arriving in Agua Caliente in roughly three hours."

Ana's brows rose. "Wow! That was fast." She grinned and stood up. Picking up her helmet, she said, "I guess I'd better pop into *tourista* clothes and go meet my counterpart."

"One more thing," Maya called.

Ana halted at the door and turned. "Yes?"

"You're in charge of this mission. Even though he's an ex-captain, you're the boss. He does what you say. I understand from our resources that Travers isn't real happy having a woman for a boss. So if he gets out of line, I want to know about it pronto. Got it?"

Tucking the helmet beneath her left arm, her Nomex gloves in her right hand, Ana murmured, "Not a problem. I'll handle it." She flipped the gloves to her brow in a mock salute to Maya. "I'll take the civilian helo in on the mining side and fly into Agua Caliente. Who do you want to have fly me in and out?"

"Have Dallas do it. She's on collateral duty today," Maya said. "And good luck. Keep your iridium phone on you at all times. If you need backup and protection, call us. We'll be on standby for you."

"Roger, Captain Stevenson. Read you loud and clear." Ana grinned widely, then turned and moved into the busy hall, toward the exit. With every step, she felt lighter and lighter. Why? It made absolutely no sense. Was it because of the unexpected assignment? It was true they worked like dogs at the base, with no downtime, no rest, no liberty. Ana had been working this arduous flight schedule for three years now.

She pushed open the door and took the metal stairs down to the first floor where another door led out into the massive cave. Then she headed for an aluminum Quonset hut at the rear, where the officers had their quarters. A quick shower, a jump into civvies and she'd be ready to go!

Smiling a little, Ana felt her heart lifting. The fact that it was Roberto's birthday today, their wedding date, had made her feel sad. It had taken an effort to fly this morning and keep her concentration sharp and focused. Her heart ached with old grief. Yet, for some reason, just seeing Jake Travers's unsmiling photo had lifted her spirits.

"Silly girl," she admonished herself as she walked through the shadowy cave. Everywhere she looked, women were working, either on the Apaches or the Cobra helicopter in maintenance, or driving the electric-powered golf carts that moved ceaselessly across the smooth, black lava surface, carrying supplies. The base reminded her of a beehive. Work went on twenty-four hours a day, seven days a week. Their mission was crucial. And they were on a wartime footing all the time.

Opening the door to the Quonset hut, Ana moved inside and down the narrow hall. Makeshift plywood cubicles had been built, each containing a small bed, a dresser and a lamp. It made for a spare, economical existence. Entering her room, Ana hung her helmet on a hook and closed the door behind her. Suddenly, she was looking forward to this unexpected mission.

It would be nice to get some time off from the brutal demands of the dangerous flight missions.

As she shimmied out of her black, Nomex uniform and prepared to take a quick shower, Ana's thoughts turned to Jake Travers. What was he really like? Did the photo lie or tell the truth? Her heart whispered that he was a caring man with a heart. *Maybe.* Ana would determine that soon enough. Miraculously, though, as she hurried down the hall to take a shower, an olive-green towel wrapped around her, she was looking forward to meeting this man. After Roberto's death, Ana had given up all hope. Love like she'd found with him could never be duplicated. She knew that. At twenty-seven, she was old enough and wise enough to know that love—deep, wonderful love— would never happen twice in a person's life.

Fatigue lapped at Jake as he sat in the restaurant. The square table before him was covered with a white linen cloth and decorated with a spray of purple orchids with red lips, set in a vase at one corner. The chef, a casually dressed man named Patrick, had had the waiter show Jake up the elegantly carved mahogany staircase to the privacy of the second floor.

Jake looked at the watch on his dark, hairy wrist. It was 11:00 a.m. Anytime now he was to meet Lieutenant Ana Lucia Cortina. Anger riffled at the edges of Jake's tiredness. He didn't want any damn woman being his commanding officer. Compressing his lips into a thin line, he sipped the fragrant and delicious mocha latte that Patrick had made for him while he waited for his contact.

Out the large windows to his left, he could see the main street of Agua Caliente, which meant "hot water," and the busy, bustling plaza beyond. The women, who were dressed in colorful skirts that hung to their ankles looked like bright tropical birds to Jake. Their hair was braided and they wore dark brown felt hats. The Peruvian men were more modern looking, although the Que'ro men wore bright red leggings and pointed, heavily beaded white caps with ear flaps. There were plenty of well-fed mongrels skulking around the plaza looking for scraps.

The plaza was rectangular, with a Catholic church of gray and black granite stonework at one end. Tourist shops that sold T-shirts, alpaca sweaters and other items, and a number of other restaurants, completed the square. Even out here, in what Jake considered the middle of nowhere, there was a pizza place! Inka pizza. With a shake of his head, he grinned a little. Amazing. Free enterprise flourished vibrantly here in Agua Caliente, from what he could see.

He heard faint footsteps on the mahogany stairs. Lifting his head, Jake set the china cup down in its saucer. He waited. It had to be Lieutenant Cortina. A hundred questions whirled through his fatigued mind. He had a black-and-white faxed photo of her, a profile shot of her in U.S. Army uniform—not really a good likeness due to the transmission difficulties of telephone lines between Peru and the U.S. Would she be a hard-ass? One of those strong, competitive women types that were in the army now? Probably.

He saw a woman, her hair black and slightly wavy as it fell around her shoulders, peek above the second floor landing. She was darkly tanned, her coloring shouting of her Peruvian heritage. Jake sucked in a breath as she turned her head and continued up the stairs, her slender hand on the rail. As she turned her oval face toward him, her cinnamon-colored eyes settled questioningly upon his. Her lips were slightly parted as if in anticipation. She looked nothing like the faxed photo of her in uniform. She was beautiful.

Without thinking, Jake rose to his feet. It was part of his officer's training to stand when in the presence of a lady. Still, he felt no woman was up to the job that lay ahead of them. Countering his irritation over Morgan's decision, he moved around the table and pulled out the chair next to his as she hesitated at the top of the stairs, looking at him. She was dressed in dark green canvas shorts, well-worn and badly nicked hiking boots, a red T-shirt that said Machu Picchu, and she wore a dark green knapsack across her shoulders. Her hair, slightly curled by the humidity, softly caressed her small breasts. Her cheeks were flushed and gave her wide, intelligent eyes even more emphasis, if that were possible.

Jake's gaze moved to her mouth. What a beautiful one she had. Her lips were full, the lower lip slightly pouty and provocative looking. A mouth made for sin. A mouth made to stir any man's fantasies. She wore absolutely no makeup, but she didn't have to, in Jake's opinion. He liked women au naturel, and she was all of that.

"Are you...?" he began awkwardly, holding out his hand. Somehow, he wished she wasn't his team partner. She was too beautiful, too feminine looking, in his judgment, to qualify for such a risky venture.

Ana smiled shyly as she stood there, her hand resting tentatively on the curved mahogany banister. "Jake Travers?" She saw him scowl as his gaze assessed her. He practically stripped her naked with his eyes. It wasn't a sexual thing, either. Ana could feel his unhappiness toward her. Like most men, he probably thought a woman couldn't do a "man's" job. Girding herself, she tried to coolly return his raking gaze, which was filled with judgment because she was a woman.

His name rolled off her lips like a lover's caress. Jake felt his skin tighten. Hell, he felt his lower body grow hot. Her soft, alto voice was like a cat's tongue licking him sinuously. He managed a curt nod. "Yeah, I'm Jake Travers. You Ana Cortina?" He sounded snarly. He felt that way.

She smiled softly and allowed his glare to glance off her. "Yes," she answered, shrugging the knapsack from her shoulders as she moved forward. How different Jake looked in real life! Ana felt her heart skipping beats, and she felt unreasonably elated at seeing him in person even if he didn't want her company. Jake was dressed in tan chinos, hiking boots, a black polo shirt that outlined the massiveness of his chest and emphasized his tightly muscled arms and broad shoulders. His hair was dark brown and cut military short. There was a slight curl to it, which gave him a less rigid look. His face was square, with a stubborn, pronounced chin. His lower lip was fuller than his upper one. Most of all, she liked his thick, dark brown brows, which lay straight across his fore-head, just above his glacial blue eyes.

She sensed his uncertainty as she approached. He even tried to smile, and her heart warmed to him immediately and without good reason. She saw surprise in his eyes, anger, and something else she couldn't quite decipher. ''Thank you,'' she whispered breathlessly as she sat down and placed the knapsack at her feet. His hand barely brushed her shoulder as he released the back of her chair. Instantly, her skin tingled. His hand was rough and calloused. Ana watched as he took his chair and sat down next to her. When he scooted it forward, his knee accidentally grazed hers.

''Sorry,'' he muttered gruffly. Jake quickly moved the chair back so they wouldn't make physical contact.

''Don't be,'' Ana murmured. She turned and saw Isidro, a Que'ro waiter, coming in their direction. He had worked for Patrick for years and was more like family to India Feliz than an employee. As he approached their table, Isidro, who was unfailingly polite, but equally shy, bowed his head and murmured a heartfelt greeting to her in Quechua, but did not meet her eyes.

Ana welcomed him warmly and ordered a mocha latte. Isidro bowed and quickly went behind the bar to the left of them to make her drink. She turned, placed her elbows on the linen tablecloth and met Jake's eyes as he assessed her with more than a little anger and some curiosity. The dark shadow of beard on his face gave him the lethal look of a warrior, Ana decided.

"Well? Do I meet with your approval?" she asked lightly.

Taken aback by her bluntness, Jake sat up straight and scowled. Ana had accurately read his mind. Shaken, he muttered, "That remains to be seen. I'm not happy about *any* woman being on this mission." Inwardly, he chastised himself for sounding grumpy and defensive. He saw shadows beneath her shining, smiling eyes and wondered if she was tired. She looked it.

Ana decided not to reply to his comment directly. She felt his tension and wariness toward her. "You were staring at me, Mr. Travers. Here in Peru, it's considered insulting to stare. Just so you know in future, because where we're going, we'll be talking to a lot of Quechua people in order to try and track down your sister. You might as well get steeped in our customs now, rather than later."

Though he was smarting beneath her gentle remonstration, Jake realized he liked her low, unruffled tone more than he should. At least Lieutenant Cortina knew how to slap a person's hand gently instead of gigging them with anger and an undiplomatic word or two. He longed to reach out and slide his fingers through her hair. The thought caught him by complete surprise. She certainly was beautiful with that thick, ebony cloak of hair about her shoulders. He had noticed she stood at around five feet ten inches tall and she had meat on her bones, wide hips and long legs. The sense of steel and strength that surrounded her was palpable. There was nothing obvious about her being a combat helicopter pilot; indeed, she looked like a tourist except for the color of her skin, which made her look decidedly Peruvian.

"I'll do my best to fit in," he mumbled.

Chuckling, Ana lifted her head as Isidro brought her drink on a silver tray. She thanked him effusively and he waited for their food order. She turned to Jake. "Hungry?"

He was. How did she know? Her eyes sparkled and she looked as if she knew him inside out. That bothered him. Rubbing his flat, hard stomach, he said, "Yeah, I'm like a starving bear."

Laughing, Ana said, "Or maybe a starving condor, down here. Do you like fresh trout? It's the specialty of the house. Patrick sends Isidro down to the Urubamba River, just a quarter of a mile from here, to fish every morning."

Jake nodded. "Then it's really fresh." He liked the warmth that glimmered in Ana's eyes. There was no hardness evident in her, just soft, inviting feminine energy. He began to relax a little, glad that she wasn't going to come at him with brute force, like some women in the military might. But that same softness made an alarm go off inside him. She couldn't possibly be up to the task ahead of them. She'd be a liability.

"Want to risk some local food?" Ana challenged him. She liked the way he was slowly releasing that hard outer shell. She saw a bit of hope burning in his light blue eyes. His mouth was softening at the corners, too. *Good.* Ana felt his nervousness and tension.

Maybe it was from the five-hour flight down here. Or maybe he was overwhelmed with worry about his sister. It could be all those things, and Ana was more than willing to let his gruffness and growliness slide off her shoulders.

"Yeah. Why not?" Wincing inwardly, Jake didn't even like himself right now. He was really being nasty toward her and she'd been the epitome of warmth and welcome. Sometimes he was a real bastard.

"*Trucha,* it is," she said, and gave Isidro their order. The waiter smiled shyly and left.

Trucha, Jake knew, was Spanish for trout. Every time Ana looked at him, he felt a little more of his nagging worry dissolving. As she delicately sipped the mocha latte, he saw an expression of enjoyment cross her face.

"Mmm, you have *no* idea how much I look forward to a little R and R here at Patrick's restaurant. And if his bed and breakfast is full, I stay at Gringo Bill's Hostel just across the plaza. Margarieta Kaiser is the owner and opens her arms to us. She knows how to take care of a war-weary soul."

"From what I understand, you're on a wartime footing at the base you fly out of all the time."

Ana nodded. She set the cup down and curved her slender fingers around it. "Yes, we are." She lifted her head and held his frank gaze. "And doing this is a very nice departure from my daily duties." Sobering, she added quietly, "I'm very sorry to hear about your sister, Mr. Travers...."

"Call me Jake, will you?" He wanted to keep her

at arm's length, but somehow, it wasn't working. A less formal atmosphere might make up for his growly attitude, he hoped.

She brightened. "Okay…you can call me Ana. All right?"

"No problem." And it wouldn't be at all for Jake. She was going to do away with military formality and that was just fine with him. He was mesmerized by the graceful movements of her hands. She was like a ballet dancer, not a combat pilot. He wrestled with the two disparate images and simply could not fit them together. Picturing her in the front seat of a deadly Boeing Apache was hard to do. Still, Jake could see her warrior side in her eyes. They were alert and missed nothing. She might be able to fight in the sky, but on the ground? No, he didn't think she was cut out for this mission at all.

"So, tell me about your sister, Jake. Do you have a photo of her?"

He reached into his back pocket and drew out his wallet. "Yeah, right here." He pulled it out and laid it on the table for her to look at.

"Oh, she's very pretty," Ana murmured as she studied the photo. Her eyes crinkled and she looked over at him. She saw grief burning in his eyes instead of the glowering anger she'd seen there before. "You're a very handsome brother and sister."

Heat trailed up his neck. Jake was blushing. Avoiding her teasing look, he paid attention to his latte and took a huge, scalding gulp. Ana Lucia Cortina was rattling him in ways he'd never anticipated. She was beautiful. Drop-dead gorgeous, with long, fine legs, a husky, warming laugh that went through him like fine whiskey, loosening him up, relaxing his knotted gut and making his heart pound and jump in his chest whenever she shared that intimate look with him. All of that told him she would be excess baggage on this mission. A pretty bauble, nothing more—and a definite liability.

"Tal's the beauty. I'm more the frog in the pond compared to her," Jake managed to reply uncomfortably.

Ana grinned. "You're very modest. How wonderful. In a *norteamericano* that is a plus." She laughed gently so as not to offend him. His cheeks had turned a dusky red color and Ana realized he was blushing. That made her like him even more, and assured her her heart was right: she'd intuited a special sensitivity in Jake and she hadn't been wrong. Not many military men she knew blushed. And it was comforting to her that Jake had that capacity. Maybe he wasn't going to be hard to work with after all—even if she was his boss.

Chapter Three

"So, your sister was working in the village of Huayllabamba when she was taken?" Ana opened up a small map and spread it across the table. They'd just eaten their fill of the pink-fleshed trout, and Isidro had cleared all the dishes away.

Jake's knee accidentally brushed Ana's as he sat forward to study her map. Again. He moved it. His left elbow splayed out on the linen tablecloth and brushed her right arm. He moved it. Somehow, his emotions, his yearnings and his worry for his sister were all becoming jumbled up inside him in one large, confused ball of sensitized nerves. Every time Ana looked at him, he melted inwardly. Her eyes were so full of life, laughter and kindness. He could feel her compassion toward him over Tal's disappearance. It wasn't an act. She understood. Still, Jake held his feelings in check. Just because she showed him a little warmth and compassion didn't mean she was suited for this mission.

"Yes," he muttered, scowling as he angled his chair so he wouldn't keep bumping her. Touching Ana was a delicious and unexpected gift to Jake. He hadn't expected to be drawn so powerfully to Ana especially now, with Tal's life on the line. "I talked to the executive vice president of the Wiraqocha Foundation and she said Tal was going to be working with six different villages, looking for water and the best place to sink a well for each. Huayllabamba was the third village on her list. That's where she disappeared."

"I see," Ana murmured. She tried to ignore the pleasant tingles on her knee and arm where Jake had accidentally brushed her. The turmoil in his pale blue eyes told her he was stressed and worried.

Tracing the black lines on the map with her slender index finger, Ana said, "This is a map of Machu Picchu and Rainbow Valley area. They are inseparable. The neck of the valley spills into the jungle, dropping from fourteen thousand to six thousand feet to intersect with the Machu Picchu Reserve. A reserve is like a national park—it's a protected area."

She tapped the map with her finger. "See this? It is our railroad—our lifeline, the only way to get in and out of Machu Picchu from Rainbow Valley, unless you want to fly in or out by helicopter." Her eyes crinkled and she looked up and met Jake's attentive gaze.

A sheet of warmth spread through her. Did she see longing in his eyes? Impossible. Ana decided she was more starved for a man's company than she'd realized. That was all it was, she told herself silently. Just an instant attraction that would dissolve as quickly as it had sparked between them. He was still grousing whenever he found an opportunity, insisting that no woman should be on a mission like this, but she ignored his grumbling.

"We can take the train from the depot down the street to Kilometer 88. The train stops there briefly every day. We can get off, then cross the mighty Urubamba River by foot, on a rope bridge to the other side. There we can pick up the Inka Trail and head toward Huayllabamba. The trail parallels another river, Rio Cusichaca. We'll be climbing from six thousand to nine thousand feet in order to reach Huayllabamba. What was the next village on her route?"

Jake unfolded a piece of paper from his pocket and spread it open. "Here's her full itinerary. Most of the place names I can't even pronounce."

Laughing softly, Ana studied the handwritten list. "Hmm, after Huayllabamba, she was to go to Paucarcancha and then Pulpituyoc, where there is a temple site. These are all located along the Inka Trail."

"What *is* the Inka Trail?"

Ana lifted her head. She saw Jake frowning as he intently studied the route she'd laid out. "It was created hundreds of years ago by the Inkas as a path between Rainbow Valley and Machu Picchu. Both places were important centers to the Inka empire. It's made up of carefully cut stones that have been placed on a path about a meter wide. The stones are about the size of a modern-day brick, usually, but there are larger ones, too.''

''A lot of labor went into it, then,'' Jake said. He liked the way Ana's mouth moved. The corners naturally flexed upward; that told him she laughed and smiled a lot. More and more of his tension and anxiety were dissolving beneath her very capable manner and her gentleness. Again, Jake found it tough to imagine Ana being a combat helicopter pilot. But then, he also admitted he didn't have a clue about the complex makeup of any woman. Especially someone like Ana. Still, he was powerfully drawn to her and wanted to know more about her on a personal level. The mission was in the way, though. And his heart was with Tal. He had no business being even mildly curious about Ana as a woman.

Chuckling, Ana said, ''You could say that. So, do we have a plan? We'll get our gear in order and hop the train?'' She looked at her watch. ''It's a little after noon. There's one leaving in about twenty minutes, and we can make that if we walk fast. The train station is about a half a mile from here. Ready?''

Jake nodded and stood. He automatically went over and pulled out the chair for Ana. She blushed beautifully over his courtly manners. He liked the slumberous quality he saw in her cinnamon eyes as she rose.

''Thank you, Jake. That was very unexpected and kind of you.''

He grinned a little shyly. ''Chivalry isn't dead, after all," he murmured, shrugging on his pack. "White knights still exist. At least, in the form of a U.S. Army officer." He saw Ana place her pack on her chair and open it up. She withdrew a beautiful handwoven scarf of brilliant rainbow colors. Placing it around her neck, she knotted it gently so that it hung between her breasts.

"That's beautiful. What is it?"

Ana closed her knapsack. When she started to put it across her shoulders, Jake quickly picked it up and held it so that she could easily slide her arms through it. His fingers brushed her shoulder. Her skin tingled. "Thank you," she said a little breathlessly. As she headed for the stairs, she said, "It's my *chalina.* I don't know if they told you of my background," she said, taking the stairs quickly, with Jake fast on her heels. "I was born in Ollytatambu, at the end of Rainbow Valley. My mother is of the Que'ro bloodline, the last of the Inkas. She is a *laykka,* a healer. And when I was growing up, she taught me to weave, as all daughters are taught the art."

At the bottom of the stairs, Ana waved goodbye to Patrick and moved out of the restaurant and down the concrete walk toward the main thoroughfare of Agua Caliente. It was glutted with tourists from around the world. Jake quickly caught up to her and walked at her shoulder, his head cocked toward her as she continued to talk.

"Every teenage girl makes her own *chalina.* They are always of rainbow colors because my people believe the rainbow is the two-headed snake of creation." She picked up the flowing end of the woven alpaca. "When a young Quechua woman decides that she is ready for a sexual relationship and marriage, she wears this. It is a sign that she will consider an offer from a young man of her choice. When she finds the man she wants to love, she will place the scarf about his neck and let him know that she wants to commit to a long, serious relationship with him. If the young man accepts, then they go off and consummate their relationship. Afterward, they visit each of the parents' homes and tell them of their commitment to one another. Both families must approve of their intention."

Jake raised his brows. They moved quickly down the concrete highway, weaving in and out of the heavy human traffic. On either side, one- and two-story homes stood. Natives dressed in colorful clothing walked in the crowds selling T-shirts, jewelry and other tourist items. "I don't think your tradition would get very far in the States."

Ana laughed pleasantly. She absorbed Jake's interest and attention. She had just spent a year without any male company and was beginning to understand how starved she'd become for conversation with the opposite sex. Men and women were different, and she enjoyed those differences. "Maybe it should. At least we are more open and honest about wanting to love another person." She patted the *chalina* gently as it swayed back and forth with her quick stride. "We don't sneak around, either. It's a very open, aboveboard signal. No guesswork." She grinned. "And it puts the emphasis on long-term commitment. This is not a roll in the hay, as I suspect you think."

Jake had the good grace to blush. "I didn't say that." By now they were crossing the plaza. Every town in Peru, he understood, had one. It was a central meeting place for the entire community and was bordered on all four sides by buildings. The cathedral was made out of gray and black granite stones, all carefully cut and laid. A testament to Inka ingenuity and skill, the stone wall was smooth and beautiful looking.

"Knowing what I know of *norteamericanos,*" Ana said impishly, "your people have very puritan views of human sexuality and sensuality. Down here in South America, we honor a woman's beauty in every way, and we also embrace our sexuality as well. It's not a taboo or dirty thing to be hidden or be ashamed of. And we don't go around rutting like sheep, either. The Que'ro way of using the *chalina* signals openly a young woman's desire. Before that, she has not had sex with anyone. So you see, it's a very monogamous ideal and has tradition at the heart of it."

Jake nodded. "I can see that. So is that why *you* are wearing it?" They moved through the square and down a hard-packed dirt slope. On his left was the roaring Urubamba River, on his right, several government buildings painted salmon and robin's-egg blue. As they reached the bottom of the hill, Ana led him up another hill that was lined with stalls and sellers. Up ahead, he saw the train station.

"I wear it because it is a sign that I am a local. I am not a gringo. When we go into this village and I speak in Quechua to the people to try and find out information about your sister, they'll not mistake me for an outsider." She dug the toes of her leather boots into the hard dirt road and moved quickly toward the train station. There was a large roofed-in area, and two trains sitting on the tracks. A concrete slab provided a place for passengers to rest their luggage before boarding.

At the train office, Ana bought two tickets, handing over the soles, the Peruvian currency, necessary for the purchase. She turned and gave Jake his ticket. "We have to hurry...." she said a little breathlessly, and jogged around the building toward the first train. Jake hurried after her. They hopped on board. Ana spotted the last two seats available, in the back. As he moved toward the seat, Jake noticed the train was filled with tourists from many nations. After placing his and Ana's packs in the overhead metal rack, he sat down beside her. Room was sparse and he was large. There was a European couple speaking German next to them, so he squeezed his bulk in, right against Ana. He had no choice. She didn't seem to mind his nearness. Like a hungry wolf, Jake secretly absorbed her tall, firm body and the warmth of her skin against his. He shouldn't enjoy it so much, he told himself sternly, under the circumstances.

The train jerked and started. It slowly began to leave Agua Caliente. Very quickly, it clickety-clacked into the jungle, following the Urubamba. Jake watched as Ana gently fingered the alpaca scarf with her lean, graceful hand. Knowing this wasn't the time or place to speak of their mission, he decided to ask her personal questions instead. Anyone eavesdropping would not be any the wiser.

"So, you come from a Que'ro family? A family of healers?"

Ana enjoyed his strength and warmth against her. It was a good thing Jake couldn't read her mind, because she was absorbing his very male energy into herself and her heart. How she missed talking with a man! She hadn't realized how much until now. Before, she'd had Roberto, whom she met at least once a month for a weekend down in Lima, and they would chatter like two parrots to one another about so many things. Ana was now beginning to understand just how much she missed him. And when she saw the burning sincerity in Jake's pale blue eyes, she knew she would lap up each moment of his attention like a cat being served a warm saucer of milk.

"My mother's family has owned land in Rainbow Valley for generations. They are *campesinos,* farmers, close to the land and to Pachamama."

"Pachamama?"

She smiled fondly. "Peruvian for Mother Earth. My people have a mystical and spiritual connection to all of nature." Ana pointed upward at the green hills. "In a little while, you will see a beautiful *apu,* a mountain with a living spirit who resides in it. We believe that the *apus* are powerful guardians and keepers of our ways. Each morning, I was taught to take three perfectly formed dried coca leaves and blow into them, to honor our local *apus*. I would then bury the coca leaves in the soft, warm earth. It is called the Andean way, today. And it's about honoring Mother Earth, all of nature—living in sync with them, not against them."

"It sounds like your people have a very spiritual tie to the earth." He saw the passion in her eyes as she spoke of what she believed in. Jake could almost see Ana sliding her long, slender fingers into the warmth of the dark, fertile earth. Just that thought sent heat tunneling through his lower body. How he'd like to be touched like that. The thought was unbidden. Moist. Full of promise. Frowning, he wondered what spell Ana was casting over him.

"Is this your first time to Peru, Jake?"

"Yes."

"I see…. The people who farm are known as *campesinos,* as I said. I come from such stock, although my father is a very rich businessman, an art collector and dealer. He met my mother when he was in the Rainbow Valley looking for woven textiles to put in his galleries in Cusco and Lima." Ana lifted her *chalina* and said softly, "He fell in love with my mother's beautiful weaving ability, but even more with her. They called her the Inkan princess because she was so beautiful. All the *campesinos* said that she would one day give her *chalina* to a very rich lord. Her beauty was such that in the old days of the Inka empire, a woman like her would be taken to Cusco, to the main temple, to marry a nobleman."

Fingering the scarf gently, Ana said, "It's such a beautiful story that I love to tell it. My father bought every blanket my mother had ever woven. He came back every month on the pretense of seeing how she was coming on future textiles for his galleries. Here in Peru, when a man wants to court a woman and she has not given him her *chalina,* he may come and serenade her with song. My father, Eduardo, played the *charango,* an Andean mandolin made of wood, and he would sing to her as she wove on the porch of her home.

"And, over a year's time, with visits each month, my father would talk endless hours with my mother about so many, many things. He was a city dweller, and she was tied to Pachamama and the ways of her people. He respected her for that and didn't want to change her at all. One day, when he arrived, he brought her a doll." Ana's eyes sparkled as she looked over at Jake, who was hanging on every huskily spoken word.

Surprised, he said, "A doll? A man brings the woman he loves a doll?"

Ana laughed, her teeth white and even. "It's a special doll, Jake. Around the doll's neck was a letter with all his credentials written down on it. He told of his heritage, his family, of his financial worth, of what he owned and most of all, how he felt toward my mother. The man speaks of love in that letter, and what he will do to always honor the woman he loves, care for her and their children. He writes of his dream, his hope, for their future."

"Well? What happened when your mother saw the doll?"

Ana grinned. "My mother was not one to fall head over heels for anyone. She's a very practical person. You see—" Ana gestured toward the window and the hills covered in jungle growth above them "—if you are a *campesino,* you are hard-working, practical and sensible. My mother took the doll, thanked him and told him to go away. That he could come back in a month if he wanted.''

''The poor guy,'' Jake murmured. ''That was a little heavy-handed, wasn't it? He'd come all the way from Cusco with this doll? And he'd probably written his heart out on that paper and she just airily told him to take a walk?''

Chuckling indulgently, Ana whispered wickedly, ''She wasn't turning him down, Jake. It is part of the elaborate ceremony, the dance between two people. She was testing his mettle, his desire to really be serious and responsible toward her. If he came back, then that would tell her of his commitment to her.''

''Obviously, he came back.''

Ana's smile widened and her eyes sparkled. ''Oh, yes. And I was the result.'' She patted her heart region gently. ''A very much loved gift to them.''

''You have any other sisters and brothers?''

''No, I'm an only child. My mother wished for more, but as a *laykka,* she had a dream, and in it, a female Apu spirit told her that her creation energy would be funneled into helping cure the sick and ailing. This she understood, so she was complete with me.''

''And your father? I'll bet he dotes on you.''

Nodding her head, she whispered, ''I love them both, so very much. I really honor my dad, who came and lived at my mother's family home. He ran his businesses from Rainbow Valley because in his letter to my mother, he swore to never take her from the land that had created her. He saw how very much she was attached to Pachamama and he in no way wanted her unhappy. He knew she'd never survive in a city environment. I love him so much for that.''

"So, you grew up a farm girl?'' Jake smiled, thinking of her as a young girl planting and harvesting crops seasonally in Rainbow Valley. He could see the earthiness in Ana. He felt it. She was hotly sensual, a quality radiating from her like the sun that gave life to all things. He liked the softness of her expression as he asked the question. The gentle rocking of the train car created a comforting motion, almost like being in someone's arms.

"My hands were in the earth, my head in the sky, as my mother used to say.''

"And where did you get this urge to fly?'' Jake wondered.

Her eyes grew merry. "I'll tell you a story you probably won't believe, but it's true. When I was three years old I remember running through the freshly dug furrows of our fields where the *campesinos* were working, my arms outstretched, trying to 'fly.' Well, one day I ran to the end of the field, which had yet to be plowed by our oxen. My mother was out with the rest of the women, feeding the men at lunchtime when it happened.'' Ana's voice grew low with emotion.

"Out of nowhere, four condors landed only a few feet away from me. I remember this incident. And I remember my mother walking slowly and quietly up to where I was standing and gawking at these huge, beautiful birds. She leaned down and whispered to me to talk to them. I remember waving my arms and saying, 'I want to fly! I want to fly with you!'''

Jake grinned. "Incredible. Do condors usually land that close to people?"

"No." Ana laughed. "Just the opposite. They live in the high, craggy and inaccessible spots deep in the Andes, where no people can reach them. They avoid humans."

"Then this was important?" Jake guessed.

Closing her eyes and leaning back against the dark green, plastic seat, Ana sighed. "Oh, yes, very important. My mother, being a *laykka,* understood its importance. As soon as I said 'I want to fly,' the four condors took off after lumbering quite a distance and flapping their wings. It's very hard for them to land on flat earth and then to take off from it. Usually, they'll land on a high crag, leap off it and float on the updrafts created. I stood there crying as they left, and my mother picked me up and held me. She said I would learn to fly like them, that although my heart belonged to Pachamama, my spirit belonged to the condors, the guardians of the air."

Ana pulled out a leather thong from beneath her T-shirt, on one end of which was a small golden disk. In a lowered tone, she told him, "In here is part of the feather of the condor that was left behind from their visit with me. My mother picked up the feather, bought the locket and placed it inside. She told me it was my medicine, my protection, and to never be without it."

"And you wear it to this day?"

"Always." Ana slanted a glance at his serious face as she slipped the locket back beneath her T-shirt. "You don't look at me like I'm *loco.* Crazy. Why?

Most *norteamericanos* would roll their eyes and call what I just told you ridiculous, say that it couldn't happen.''

Shrugging, Jake studied her thoughtful, upturned face. Her eyes were so warm and alive, the color of rich, recently turned soil. ''Maybe because I'm a farmboy from Iowa? My parents have a huge corn and soybean farm, and I grew up with dirt under my nails just like you did.'' He watched her eyes widen beautifully. His heart wrenched. There was such an incredible array of emotions that raced across Ana's vulnerable features, and he could read each one. He was amazed at her openness and accessibility. And then it struck him that Ana trusted him. Deeply. Shaken by that discovery, he found himself wanting to open up to her more, too. But could he? Did he dare? No, he was afraid to because of his hurting, scarred past. Besides, he had to hold back. Had to remember he had been teamed up with her to complete a mission he didn't think she—or any woman— was capable of.

''You are a *campesino* at heart!'' Ana whispered, sitting up. She slid her fingers through her loose black hair and turned toward him, one leg beneath her and her knee pressed up against his massive, jean-clad thigh. ''How wonderful! What are the chances I would ever meet a man like you? This is incredible!''

Warming beneath her appreciation, her effusive, ebullient joy, Jake avoided her awestruck gaze. When he felt her hands on his left arm, a wild, unbidden energy and heat moved up his shoulder and into his chest, finally reaching his opening heart. No matter what he did, he could not remain immune to Ana. She was so childlike in her innocence toward him, and toward life in general. And that was what drew him dangerously to her. She trusted him without reserve. She shouldn't.

"Whoa," he cautioned, holding up his hand. "Don't read too much into this, okay?"

"Why not?" Ana pouted provocatively as she saw his discomfort over her touching him. Wisely, she released his thick, hard-muscled arm and sat back in the seat to observe Jake more closely. She saw desire in his eyes—for her. Ana felt it flow into her heart and lift her wafting spirits. So why was Jake backing off? Why did she feel him retreating in a panic? She had no answers. Patience was not her strong point, yet she knew she had to practice it with this *norteamericano*.

"Because..." he began in a strained tone.

She laughed softly. "I'm scaring you. Okay, I'll back off."

He met her teasing look. Feeling sheepish, Jake muttered, "You read minds, too?"

"No, but I'd like to think I'm sensitive to facial expressions and body language."

"Touché."

Jake almost said the words: *You're too soft, too beautiful for this mission.* Somehow, he swallowed them, but a lump remained in his throat.

Chapter Four

Once off the train, Ana enthusiastically greeted the station master in Quechua. She and Jake were the only people to get off at Kilometer 88. Jake couldn't make out a word she was saying as she disappeared into the small rock hut with a thatched roof behind the train master, an old man who was bent over, probably from carrying very heavy loads all his life.

Jake looked around him. Directly across the tracks and down a steep, grassy embankment was a swinging rope bridge across the wild Urubamba River. The roar of the water filled the area. The day was growing to a close, the sun sinking behind the mountains. Turning, he could see the whitish-gray stones on the other side of the river and figured this path must be the Inka Trail system.

"Jake?" Ana called. "Come here. Come and get your trail pack."

Turning, he saw her carrying two large packs on solid aluminum frames. Surprised, he took one. "Where did you get these?"

She smiled and hefted one forty-pound pack across her shoulders, shifting it across her hips to tighten the belt around her waist. "My friend here, Macedo, is the leader of a nearby village. He is responsible for taking care of this stop on the train route. When I get a chance, I like to hike the trail, to get back to nature after flying in an Apache all the time." She adjusted the thick shoulder pads and settled them against her body, giving Jake a brief smile. "Usually, one of my women friends goes with me, so we keep two packs here for any time off we get for a little R and R. Which isn't often." She turned and graciously thanked Macedo, who bowed a number of times to her.

Arranging her colorful scarf around her neck, Ana straightened and breathed in the moist, pure air. "It's so beautiful here," she murmured. Giving Jake an impish look, she added, "And I'm glad to share it with you. Are you about ready to cross that rickety old bridge?"

Jake nodded, but felt hesitant. He had strapped on the second large pack, which held a rolled-up sleeping bag and, he was sure, other items for camping. Looking up at the sky, he noticed stormy clouds were beginning to gather. "Yeah, I am. Think it's going to rain?"

"You can count on it. We're in the mountains, at

eight thousand feet, and weather here turns on a dime.'' Ana brushed past him, leaped off the concrete block that was the station platform, to the gravel and rails. Jake followed.

The bridge was made of thick white hemp, hand-woven to provide access across the roaring, frothing Urubamba. Ana stopped short of the bridge and dug into her pocket. She produced some dried green leaves in a plastic bag. Holding them up as Jake came to her shoulder, she said, ''These are coca leaves. I'm going to make an offering and pray to the *apus* and the river *nust'a*—goddess—for a safe crossing.''

Jake nodded. He had no problem with her belief system and he watched, fascinated, as Ana chose three perfectly formed, dried leaves and arranged them like a small fan between her thumb and index finger. Turning, she faced the mountain, which was hidden by the hills, and held the leaves to her lips and blew gently on them. Then she turned to the four points of the compass and did the same thing. Bending down, she dug into the moist, rich earth and buried the leaves. Patting the soil gently, as a mother would her child, she stood and smiled at him.

''The Quechuan people live with nature. We are a part of it, not separated like many other people are. I said prayers and asked for a safe crossing, and also honored the *apus* so that our journey would be swift and sure.''

''Not a bad idea,'' Jake murmured as he watched the clouds above them thicken, twist and become pregnant with rain. Ana quickly moved onto the rope bridge, her hands grasping the rope sides to steady herself. She moved like a nimble deer on the hand-cut wooden planks that served as steps across the chasm below. When Jake stepped onto it, he discovered just how unsteady it was. Ana had made it look easy. However, thanks to his ranger training, he was used to negotiating tricky obstacles like this, and in no time he was at her side.

Ana smiled triumphantly at him. "You're an old hand at this, Jake."

He grudgingly warmed beneath the dazzling look in her shining eyes. Ana made him feel strong and good about being a man. She made him feel like he was walking on air when she gave him that artless, enthusiastic smile of hers. "Thanks. You're no slouch yourself." And she wasn't—but that didn't mean she could help him. Ana might be useful on this part of the mission, but not when it came to the kind of dangers they would encounter in rescuing Tal.

Chuckling, Ana scrambled up the well-trodden path to the white brick road, the Inka Trail. "I was born and raised here, remember? This is familiar territory to me."

As he made his way to the trail and stood at her side, she said, "Welcome to the internationally famous Inka Trail. You're treading where Inka runners have passed for nearly a thousand years." She tapped her foot on the smooth, white-gray stones, which had been perfectly set against one another to make a seamless path.

Jake looked both ways along the curving, sloping trail, which was surrounded by tall, stately eucalyptus trees. The various hues of the green and silver leaves were beautiful. "I like history," Jake told her. "If we can learn from what happened in the past, we're better off."

"Mmm, a philosopher, too," Ana said with a gleam in her eyes as she took his hand and tugged on it. "Come on, I'd like to get started before it starts to pour. We'll try to spend the night at Pacamayo. It's a large, well-situated camp. We'll probably run into a lot of *tourista* groups there, but I don't want to try to hike Abra de Huarmhuanusca—Dead Woman's Pass—today."

Jake raised his brows. "Dead Woman's Pass? What kind of a name is that?" He felt her hand slip free of his. Instantly, he missed Ana's soft, firm touch. If they weren't on a mission, Jake would have been happy just to walk the Inka Trail holding her hand, as there was plenty of room for two people to walk side by side.

"The legend goes that a woman died up there, praying for the spirit of her lover, who had died in a fall. A storm came and she was struck by lightning. The *campesinos* fear lightning, and so the name stuck. When it happened, no one remembers. It's a very ancient legend. The pass is 4200 meters high. There are steps leading up to this first mountain pass, thank goodness—built in 1998 by the Peruvian Government, so they aren't really part of the historical Inka Trail. But it does make the traverse a lot easier and faster now."

Ana set a quick pace, and Jake was impressed with her physical speed and endurance. As he walked at her shoulder, he saw about fifteen people coming their way, all tourists. In back of them were Que'ro Indians, small, hardy, dark brown people with huge loads wrapped in colorful blankets on their bent backs. Ana moved off the trail and Jake followed her. They murmured a greeting to the leader, a man from Germany, it seemed, and his all-German tourist group.

Jake saw that the tourists carried hiking sticks, but very little gear. The Que'ro porters, on the other hand, were carrying heavy loads, of everything including the kitchen sink. When the lead Que'ro saw Ana, his face creased in a wide smile. He quickly spoke to her in Quechua, and she replied. The porters all nodded deferentially to them, and each in turn spoke enthusiastically to Ana. Jake guessed the packs they were carrying probably weighed close to a hundred pounds a piece, and yet these sturdy men with knotty calves who were less than five feet five inches tall, handled them amazingly well. He liked their colorful clothing, especially their beaded caps with ear flaps, woven in bright red, orange, yellow, black and pink. They wore tight-fitting red breeches to just below their knees, and open-toed sandals made out of car tires.

After they trooped by, Jake said in a low tone, "They're carrying a lot of weight on their backs for those tourists."

Ana nodded. "The porters are strong, Jake. They take pride in how much they can carry."

He grinned mischievously. "Why don't the *touristas* carry their own weight? Isn't this what it's about? Hiking the Inka Trail? Not going out for a Sunday walk in the park and letting others do their dirty work."

She laughed with him and moved quickly back onto the trail, her stride long and rhythmic. "Yes, well, that's the joke in Rainbow Valley, which we're in now. *Touristas* are rich and can afford to have others carry their load. At least," Ana said, losing her smile, "the money the porters earn helps their families, and that's the important thing. There are parts of the Inka Trail that are dangerous, and sometimes a porter will slip and fall to his death. It's a terrible thing to lose a member of a village. It's like losing a loved one, because the *ayllu,* or Andean community, is like an extended family. Everyone works together. Everyone sings and dances and gets drunk together. We share everything. When an *ayllu masa*—a member of our community—dies, we all feel it. We all grieve as one."

"You have a family and community closeness that we had in North America back in the 1800s, before we started spreading out from one coast to another," Jake observed, studying her as she walked beside him. Ana's hair was becoming more crinkled because the humidity was increasing. The long, wavy black strands slid across her shoulders as she continued up the trail. Her cheeks were flushed pink, and yet she was breathing easily. He, on the other hand, was not breathing well at all and found himself huffing. It had to be the altitude.

"Yes, I've studied American West history extensively," Ana said, glancing up at Jake. "But now, you are community-less. Your family unit is no longer tightly knit. People within your small towns and large cities do not know or help one another."

She waved her hand in front of her. "Our way of life has endured for thousands of years. The Inkas, when they came to power, realized the beauty of our Andean system, and supported and enhanced it. When the Spanish came in 1500, they tried to destroy what we had, but no matter what they did, we survived it." Ana grinned. "Today, our Andean ways are stronger than ever."

"Adversity made you strong," Jake said. More and more he was admiring Ana and her people. He wanted to tell her that she was a wonderful ambassador. Seeing the world through her eyes was invigorating and exciting to him. Jake had never expected to have a partner like her on a mission like this. With her laughter and her open heart, she took the edge off his constant worry about Tal.

"Exactly," Ana said. She cocked her head and gave him a sober look. "Tell me about yourself. What were your growing up years like? You are a *campesino* at heart, no? Your parents have a corn farm in Iowa?" She liked the way his mouth softened when she spoke to him. Even though he was obviously a hardened warrior used to the brutal circumstances of his training and work as a U.S. Army Ranger, Ana saw a wonderfully sensitive side to Jake. And a lot of his icy gruffness from earlier was gone, too. Maybe she was showing him that she was a worthwhile member on this mission and this allowed him to open himself to her. Whatever the reason, she found her heart responding joyfully to his growing trust in her.

"Not much to tell," he murmured. "I come from three generations of farmers. I have two other brothers, and Tal, of course, and they all left the farm, too. My dad has had trouble meeting his debts, so the four of us left to get better paying jobs, and we send money home so he and Mom can keep our homestead. Corn prices have really sagged in the last decade, and my folks would have lost the farm if we hadn't left to work elsewhere.''

"I see…. Did you *want* to leave?'' Ana pointed to his large, square hands, seeing the thick yellow calluses on his palms. "You have earth hands, Jake.'' She splayed hers out before him, her fingers long and tapered. "See? Square hands. It's a sign that you belong to Mother Earth.'' And she smiled up at him.

He returned her smile hesitantly. "I've never thought of it that way. Yeah…I guess if I got a chance, I'd go back to the land. I liked it. I liked plowing the fields, the planting. I like being outdoors.'' Jake glanced upward. Overhead, the clouds, swollen with rain, were growing a gunmetal gray. The wind was picking up, becoming sharp sometimes and tugging at them restlessly.

"And you love the army, too? Because it's an outdoor job?'' Ana met his assessing eyes. She felt her body respond fully to that hooded look Jake gave her. How could she be drawn so powerfully to him? A stranger who had walked into her life? A *norteamericano* at that? In all her life, Ana had never envisioned herself being drawn to an Anglo from the north. Yet she was.

"Yeah, I like the challenge, the brutal physical demands. And I like the competition with the elements, and with the bad guys. I guess I have this crazy notion

I'm a modern day white knight without his charger.''
He gave her a teasing grin.

''But if you could, would you go home to your
farm? Your roots?''

Nodding, Jake said, ''In a heartbeat, but that's not
going to happen now, Ana. My parents are clinging
to the land, paying a hundred-fifty-thousand-dollar
loan to the banks and if they miss a payment, the bank
will sell the farm out from under them. My other two
brothers, both older than me, are in the military, too.
Tal went to college to become a hydrologist. Among
us, we send them enough money to keep their heads
above water. It's a tough time for farmers in the
U.S.A.''

''I see… So you do what you can to stay close to
Pachamama in this way, as a ranger?''

''Well,'' Jake said sadly, ''I had to resign my commission in order to get down here to find Tal. My
commanding officer refused to give me leave to come
to Peru. So I resigned and left the army.''

''Oh, dear…'' Ana murmured. ''That was wrong.
Your C.O. should have let you come. You're an officer, a man of many talents and skills. How could he
throw you away like that?'' Ana admired Jake for his
courage, his love for his sister. He'd chosen Tal over
his job and career. That took a lot of guts, Ana knew.
It also left Jake without an income. He'd given up a
lot to find his sister.

Shrugging, Jake slowed to a stop. He was breathing
hard and fast, his heart pounding like a freight train
in his chest. Leaning over, his hands on his bent
knees, he said, ''It was a stupid decision on my C.O.'s

part, but I wasn't going to let anything or anyone stop me from coming down here to find my sister.''

''You are very like us in many, many ways, Jake. You place family, parents, land and heritage before other things.''

He snorted, bowed his head and braced against a cooling gust of wind that blasted them from behind. ''That and a dollar might get you a cup of coffee,'' he said in jest. Slowly straightening, his breath coming less harshly now as he rested, he held Ana's upturned gaze. Her eyes shone with respect for him. Once again he felt strong and good beneath her warm cinnamon eyes. What Ana felt toward him, Jake was discovering, was important to him. He *wanted* her to admire him. To think that he was a good man. Someone she could always trust, who would always be there for her if she needed him.

''What will you do after we find Tal? You have no job. No money.''

Shrugging, Jake slid his fingers beneath the thick shoulder straps and adjusted his load he carried. ''I don't really know. I have a little nest egg saved up. First things first, though. I need to find Tal. A lot depends upon her and how she is. If she's hurt…or worse…I want to be there for her however I can be….''

Ana heard the worry in his voice and saw the fear in his eyes. Reaching out, she curled her fingers around his upper arm and felt his thick, hardened muscles flex beneath her fingertips. ''We'll find her,'' she promised him huskily. ''I said a special prayer for Tal to our *apus*. They will help us find her quickly. I prayed for her safety. They will keep her safe, Jake. I know you probably think what I'm saying is crazy—'' she looked up at the hills surrounding them ''—but the spirits of nature down here are very much alive, very responsive to anyone who asks help from them.''

''Then I'm going to start asking, too.'' Her hand felt steadying on his arm. Jake stopped himself from stepping inches closer and sweeping Ana into his arms. Her hair was in disarray, tossed by the inconstant breezes. Her cheeks were a deeper pink now, and her wide, innocent eyes were lovely enough to make a man drown in them, heart and soul. Right now, Ana looked like a wild, primal part of nature, not a pilot, and certainly not a woman in the military. And that bothered him. He couldn't reconcile the two images of her. His traditional ideas, his old-fashioned expectations of her as a woman were strongly ingrained in him.

Ana released him. ''Then do it with coca leaves.'' She gave him three perfect leaves from her bag. ''Coca leaves are sacred to the *apus* and *nust'as,* the gods and goddesses of nature. If you use coca leaves and pray to them, they will listen. Just hold the leaves in your hand, close your eyes, think of Tal and ask for their help to keep her safe.''

Jake smiled a little as he carefully held the three small leaves in his large fingers. ''I'm not much for praying, Ana.'' And he wasn't. Jake wasn't sure about this mystical world she believed in, but he felt a peace here he'd never felt anywhere else he'd ever been in the world. He was a globe-trotter of sorts, because he was a ranger. Still, a little trust in her spiritual world wouldn't hurt anything, and he was willing to try anything to save Tal's life.

Ana watched as he awkwardly held the leaves in his massive hand, closed his eyes and bowed his head a little. Touched by his attempt to pray for his sister in the ways of the Andean people, she felt her heart sing. The *touristas* who came to Peru rarely wanted to know anything of her people or their ways. And too frequently, tourists laughed at her beliefs. Not Jake Travers.

As he opened his eyes, he glanced at her, a rueful look on his face. "Now what? Do I dig a hole and bury them like you did?"

Smiling gently, Ana nodded. "Yes. Just hold Tal in your thoughts. See her face. See her happy and smiling."

Moving off the trail to dig a small hole, Jake squatted down. "That won't be hard to do."

Once the leaves were buried, Jake rejoined Ana on the trail and they took off once again. Splatters of rain began to fall. Ana pointed up ahead, to a grove of stately eucalyptus trees.

"Let's stop there and set up our tents for the night. The rain gods are going to probably deluge us shortly."

When they got to the thick stand of trees, it was raining erratically. The afternoon light had faded quickly into evening, with low-hanging, angry-looking clouds now surrounding them. After Jake laid his pack down on the grass beneath the trees, he searched inside for a small tent. Ana, who knelt nearby, pulled her own tent from the bottom of her pack.

"I don't think I have a tent," he told her. The wind rose and howled in fury. The rain began in earnest.

"Oh dear..." Ana frowned. "Quick, come and help me get this tent up. We'll share it. I don't want us wet and cold at this altitude."

Jake hurriedly worked with her to erect the small nylon tent and pound stakes into place to hold it. Both quickly crawled inside it, hauling their packs in with them. There was barely room to sit up, especially for Jake because of his height. Ana squirmed around, accidentally kicking him with her boots in the tight space.

"Sorry," she murmured, quickly zipping up the entrance. Wind beat erratically against the nylon shell of the tent. Sitting up, she pushed her tangled hair off her face and smiled at him. Their quarters were really cramped. With their huge packs inside, they couldn't even turn around without bumping into one another. Her heart beat wildly. It wasn't from the altitude. No, it was from being this close to Jake. Swallowing, Ana managed another small smile. "I don't know about you, but I'm getting out of my boots. We can open our sleeping bags and get inside them to dry off and keep warm."

"Good idea," he murmured. But as he began removing his boots, Jake kept running into Ana's arm, her elbow or shoulder. A clap of thunder sounded overhead. The wind blasted through the stand of trees. Rain began pelting down in earnest.

"Do storms like this pop up often?" he asked, setting his boots aside.

Nodding, Ana tucked her own boots into a corner and then opened her pack to drag out her sleeping bag. Jake was so close. So pulverizingly masculine. She wanted to touch him the way a woman would touch her man in sensual exploration. Fighting her desires, Ana said as she laid out her bag, "Yes. We're in the mountains now, halfway between the humid, moist heat of the jungle and the cold air coming off the *apus* surrounding this valley. The hot and cold air mix, and storms pop up all the time. Especially in the late afternoon and evening hours."

By the time they had their sleeping bags laid out and were snugly wrapped in them, the storm was raging. In the dim light Jake could barely make out Ana's facial expressions. She lay on her side, her arm propping up her head, her hand resting against her jaw as she faced him. He lay in a similar position. Their voices were muted by the storm growling and snarling around them. The lightning would dance across the sky and illuminate the inside of the tent briefly. And every time, Jake would look at Ana's peaceful, serene features. Her eyes were half-closed, her soft lips parted, the corners turned upward as they talked in hushed tones. The inside of the tent was warm from their body heat.

"There's one thing I really need to know," Jake told her in a teasing manner.

"What's that?" Ana liked his low, deep voice. It moved through her like a haunting Andean flute melody, touching her core as a woman.

"I'm having one helluva time equating you, here, with the image of you as an Apache gunship pilot. How did you get mixed up with the U.S. Army? That has to be a story in itself."

Laughing softly, Ana turned onto her back and placed her hands behind her head. "Oh, yes, that is a story, Jake."

"Well, we've got all the time in the world," he observed dryly. "We aren't going anywhere until dawn tomorrow. I'm all-ears." He was hungry to know all about her. To try and understand why Morgan would allow a woman, especially Ana, to be on this dangerous mission.

Laughing softly, Ana said, "You're a glutton for punishment, then. I don't think I'm *that* interesting."

Jake checked the urge to reach out and touch her hair, which lay in an ebony coverlet about her head and shoulders. They were so close…so agonizingly close. What would it be like to hold Ana in his arms tonight? Make sweet, passionate love to her? Feel her earthy, sensual form, her arms wrapped around his shoulders? Chiding himself, Jake knew he didn't dare do such a thing. Tal's life was at stake. They could be in danger themselves on this trail. He didn't know the territory at all. No, he had to remain alert, not give his aching heart away to this incredible woman who seemed made of earth and of air, nature a vital part of her.

Sighing, Ana said, "Okay…just remember, you asked for it."

"You'll never bore me."

Giggling, Ana said, "I love your sense of humor,

Jake.'' She reached out spontaneously and patted his hand. Ana wanted to do more, but fiercely told herself that she couldn't. As much as she wanted to share herself with Jake, this wasn't the time nor the place.

Removing her hand, Ana said, ''My father was in the Peruvian Air Force before he settled down in his family's business of art dealership. His father had been a pilot, too, so he was following family tradition. Family is very important here in South America. When the condors landed in front of me as a three-year-old, my parents decided that I was meant to fly, too. My father, who was very influential in government politics, helped to create openings for women to join the Peruvian military. I was one of the first two women to be allowed to learn to fly helicopters in the Peruvian army. Because we were at the top of our class, we were sent to the U.S. Army's training center in Fort Rucker, Alabama, to learn how to fly Apache helicopters. This was a very big thing, you know...for the Peruvian military to send two women up there. Usually, male pilots were sent there for multi-national or what we call cross-training.''

''So you're really making strides for all women down here in Peru.'' Jake admired her verve and guts. He knew how hard it was for North American women to survive in the military. He couldn't even begin to imagine the harassment and pressures on Ana and the other South American woman. And then to be selected and sent to the U.S. for further training, which was always seen as a plum assignment by foreign military services, probably placed her in an envious position that her fellow pilots, the males, wouldn't like at all.

"Yes...we are role models of a sort," Ana agreed quietly. "We had a lot of trouble up at Fort Rucker with one particular flight instructor, a Captain Dane York. If it weren't for Chief Warrant Officer Maya Stevenson, he would have flunked all of us out of training just because we were women. It didn't matter that all the women pilots, despite his prejudice, were at the top of the class. He just didn't believe we could do the job as well as a man could. So Maya asked her father, who is an army general, for help. Well, Captain York mended his ways, but it left a bitter taste in the mouths of all the women pilots who were under his command.

"Maya was so angry over the injustice that she conceived a plan for a secret base here in Peru, to help stem the floodtide of cocaine being flown from our country into Bolivia, where it isn't stopped at all. Her father pushed it through. It became a spec ops—special operations. When Maya told us about it, every last woman volunteered to be part of her Black Jaguar squadron."

The lightning flashed and momentarily illuminated the tent, revealing the look of intense interest on Jake's face. She saw his brows draw down in a scowl, saw censure in his eyes when he heard about the treatment she'd received. Waving her hand, she murmured, "We came here, to a secret base in the mountains. And the rest is history. I've spent the last three years here, as has every other woman who came with Maya. We've reduced the air flights of cocaine out of

Peru in this area by fifty percent, and that's pretty good considering the drug lords have millions of dollars to throw away on the best foreign aircraft, like Kamov Black Sharks, and the best Russian combat pilots, who fly them as mercenaries, demanding only U.S. dollars for their services."

"So," Jake growled, "you're really in a war up to your hocks and back. I didn't realize that."

"Very much a wartime footing," Ana agreed somberly. The crash of thunder rolled through the grove, shaking the tent. The rain continued, furious and unabated. "But I love it. I believe in what we're doing. And Maya...well, she's an extraordinary person with unusual skills and abilities. I'd fly with her anywhere she asked me to. We're an all-woman unit, even down to the mechanics, cooks and office personnel. The army likes to ignore us. Maya caused so much trouble up at Fort Rucker that I think they were more than happy to see us all disappear down here. We weren't a PR liability to them, that way." Ana chuckled.

"So," Jake murmured, "you're a Peruvian Air Force pilot on loan to the U.S. Army?"

"Yes, exactly. I draw my pay from Peru. And frankly speaking, because I'm a woman, they don't want me in Lima, either. The Peruvian male pilots are up in arms that women are allowed to fly at all. The pilot I trained with, Lieutenant Mirella Gallardo, comes from a very rich copper-mining family in Lima and is my best friend. She's been with Maya since the beginning, too."

Jake shook his head. "You've really butted heads with men in the military." He admired Ana's spirit and spunk. More importantly, he didn't see her taking out her anger or resentment on the men around her, which spoke highly of her maturity. Maybe because she was a woman, she was able to work well with a partner in a close-knit team? Women had an innate ability to do that, from what Jake had observed.

Laughing a little, Ana said, "Oh, yes…but those of us who fly with the Black Jaguars know what is really important. What men think of us is not. Stopping the drugs from leaving the country and especially, keeping children from taking them, is the heart and soul of why we do what we do."

"And it's dangerous."

"Always."

Jake scowled. "You ever thought of…well… having a family? Where I come from…my family…women should be at home, be housewives, and mothers to our children."

Closing her eyes, Ana whispered, "Oh, yes…with Roberto—my fiancé." She opened her eyes, which were filled with sadness now. "But that is a lost dream. Roberto was killed a year ago, while aboard a Peruvian navy cruiser. He was shot down by drug runners." Blinking back the tears that threatened, she continued, "Maya knows that the women under her command are young and full of hopes and dreams. She doesn't expect us to stay with the operation forever, as she plans to. Her commitment to Peru is in her blood, in her bones and her soul. She knew that when Roberto and I married, I would leave as soon as she got a replacement pilot for me."

Jake scowled at the vulnerability he saw in Ana's

eyes. He itched to move his hand those scant few inches and find Ana's shoulder. To hold her, offer her comfort—and so much more, he admitted to himself. He wanted to kiss her. He wanted to taste her, feel her and share her delicious warmth. Shrugging off his desire, he asked instead, "And she was okay with that?"

"Of course. Maya is a red-blooded South American woman herself." Ana, chuckled, her humor returning. "Just because we are an all-woman base of operations doesn't mean we don't like men. Just the opposite! We talk about them often!"

He caught her amusement and said, "That's good. So what were your plans after you married? Settle in Lima, where Roberto worked?"

Ana lost her smile. She closed her eyes, some old pain drifting back into her heart momentarily as the sound of the rain on the roof of their tent soothed her. "I agreed to live with Roberto down in Lima until he retired from the navy, which would have been ten years from now. And then we would have come back up here, to Rainbow Valley, to live at my parents' farm. I really want to get back to my family, to Pachamama. I love the land, the seasons...and I wanted to raise our children up here, where they could be wild and free as I had been...." Her voice lowered painfully. "But that will never be, now."

"Maybe you'll fall in love again?"

Ana heard the hope in Jake's voice. Her heart swelled with need of him, but she felt scared. In a choked tone, she said, "I don't know, Jake...it's just so hard for me. My heart can't handle another loss like this. It just can't...." For whatever reason, his disgruntled demeanor made her heart open toward him. Ana had thought her heart had died when Roberto died, but to her surprise, it hadn't. This *norteamericano,* for whatever reason, gently held a key to her grieving heart. Ana was frightened and simultaneously lured by Jake. She sternly reminded herself that he was a visitor—someone who would leave as soon as his sister was found. And she would not become involved in such a transient way; her heart simply couldn't take such a beating again—ever.

Shaking his head, he muttered, "I just don't see how women can do this...."

"What?"

"Flying like you do. It's dangerous."

Ana saw that his expression was tight with judgment. "Just because I'm a woman I shouldn't be in the military? Or take part in combat?"

Hearing the edge in her voice, he sighed. "Yeah, because you're a woman. I guess all my old traditional instincts are rising to the top. My job is to protect the defenseless. I see women and children in that category."

"We've all managed to survive three years without any help from men. Maya hadn't intended it to be that way, but the army has pulled out a lot of its support of what we do, so we've basically had to make good with who and what we have."

"Don't you..." He groped for the right words. "Don't you miss being at home? Still long to get married? Have kids? Be a mother?"

She heard the disbelief in his voice. "I don't define

myself in just those roles, although someday I hope to have children and be a mother to them. No one forced you to go into the army rangers, did they?''

"No. So what?''

"So, we all choose careers that touch our heart, Jake. I love to fly. I see nothing wrong with being an Apache helicopter pilot. Just as you see nothing wrong with having been an army ranger. To me, it's not a gender question at all. To you it is.''

Thunder rolled loudly down the valley again. The tent vibrated with the noise. Jake shook his head. "I just don't think women can take the heat in combat. Maybe you get a different perspective flying as a pilot than you get as a ground pounder who sees the bleeding up close and personal.'' He slanted her a glance in the darkness. "I don't think any woman can be as good as a man in ground combat.''

Ana lay there a long time digesting his comment. Finally, she said, "Whether you like it or not, or whether you believe in my ability to hold up my end of this mission isn't the issue, Jake. You agreed to this mission with my being in command. I've tried to make you feel like an important part of this team of ours. You would not get anywhere near Tal or where she might be held prisoner if not for me.''

Glumly, Jake murmured, "I know.''

Lying on her back, her hands tucked beneath her head, Ana felt hurt weave through her heart. Jake didn't trust her. Not like she trusted him. Sighing, she closed her eyes. Tomorrow was another day. Maybe she could show her skills as a leader, and over time, Jake would come to trust her. Why did he have to be so backward about women and their abilities?

Chapter Five

Ana's last words were spoken softly and drifted off like the drumming of the rain on the roof of their small, cozy tent. As the storm passed, Jake remained awake, on his side and facing her in the complete darkness. The plop, plop, plop of rain gathering at the tips of the leaves and falling from the trees that surrounded them was soothing to Jake. He was exhausted by the flight and then having to hike at a high altitude. His body had not adjusted yet.

Though he ached to reach out those few scant inches to where Ana lay asleep in her nylon sleeping bag, Jake stifled the urge. Having been married once, he knew the delicious and overwhelming feelings of having a warm, wonderful woman's body fitting against his own. He wanted Ana in his arms. He wanted to know what she felt like against him. Her soft, shallow breathing made his heart open and throb with need. She was afraid to love again. Could he blame her? No. Didn't he feel the same way, ever since his wife had been ripped brutally from his life? And hadn't he felt only half-alive since Carol's death?

Frowning, Jake forced his eyes shut. With Ana, he felt whole once more, and that shocked and frightened him. He had never thought he'd meet another woman who even began to match Carol in personality and sensuality, but he had. Ana had stepped out of the mists of Peru, like some kind of fevered dream he'd often had that was now real. Very real. And very appealing and provocative to him, even though she was not flirting with him at all.

The rumble of thunder was now far away, moving on down the Rainbow Valley, he supposed. As exhausted as he was, Jake found his mind racing and his thoughts shifting between Ana and his missing sister. His heart warred between incredible joy and a haunting terror. Feeling as if he were on a nonstop, out-of-control roller coaster of emotions, he forced himself to go to sleep. As he drifted deeper into the arms of the Peruvian night, Ana's beautiful face gently appeared before him, her cinnamon eyes warm with laughter, her full lips slightly parted and her hand extended toward him....

Sometime near dawn, with the chirping of the first bird in a nearby tree, Jake pulled himself from the depths of sleep. His senses were fragmented. He felt the warmth of a woman in his arms. It felt familiar. Welcoming. He felt the soft moisture of her breath against the column of his neck. The weight of one arm was around his torso. Was he still dreaming of Ana? Or was this real? Fighting to awaken, Jake drowsily fluttered his lids. The tickle of hair against his chin roused him even more. The weight of someone's head resting on his right arm, a face pressed into the crook of his shoulder made him drag his eyes wide open.

Grayish light hung in the tent; it was not quite night, but not dawn yet, either. The tent was warm. The rustle of leaves told him of a slight breeze wafting through the area. A chirp of another bird pierced the sluggish dawn light. His awakened senses slowly became aware of the woman in his arms, pressed against the length of his body.

Ana lay curled up in her sleeping bag against him. Sometime during the night she had moved from her back onto her left side, and into full contact with him. Her hair lay about her like a dark, silken coverlet, some of it tickling his chin. Her brow was pressed against the hard line of his jaw. Inhaling her sweet, womanly fragrance into his flaring nostrils, Jake felt fire tunneling down through him and settling hotly in his lower body. Ana smelled wonderful to him. Luxuriating in her innocent posture, he knew that she had probably turned over in her sleep and wasn't even aware—yet—that she was in his arms. For one selfish moment, Jake wanted, like a starving wolf, to absorb her into his being.

Her right arm had slid innocently across his waist and hung limply against his back. The thick, lumpy sleeping bags created a barrier between them, but that didn't matter. Right or wrong, Jake was going to enjoy this moment. Lifting his left hand, he lightly threaded his fingers through her long, slightly curled hair. He moved the strands away from her face, exposing her high cheekbones and thick, black lashes, which lay against her gold flesh. How beautiful, how peaceful Ana looked. Jake could feel the slow rise and fall of her breasts and knew she was still deeply asleep.

The sense that Ana trusted him like this shook Jake. Maybe she was afraid to love again, but on a perhaps more primal level, she had gravitated to him, knowing intuitively that he longed thirstily for her. Closing his eyes, Jake barely touched the warm firmness of her arm. He shouldn't be doing this. He was taking advantage of Ana in her sleep. His conscience nagged him. It warred with his longing to kiss her awake. Easing up on an elbow, Jake gazed down at Ana in the growing light. Shadows moved kindly across her very Indian face. He saw nothing but beauty in Ana. She was perfect to him. The way her black hair cascaded like a dark waterfall around her shoulders, the way her full lips were slightly parted, all conspired against him and made him long for things he didn't dare long for.

The fire within him burned hotter and his lower body tightened painfully. He wanted Ana in all ways—the way a man wanted his woman. Yet the chivalry within him won out. He would not take advantage of her...not while she was asleep, at least. The last thing Jake wanted was for Ana to distrust him. No, he wanted her, but on her own terms and with her agreement. Otherwise, there would be a loss of respect between them, and that would set the vibrations between them off-kilter. Jake wanted Ana to want him fair and square. Maybe it was his upbringing on a conservative Iowa farm that won out. He wasn't sure. He'd always been taught to respect a woman and not push himself on her. Jake smiled sadly. He would have to kiss Ana in his dreams, not in real life.

"Hey…" He called softly, leaning down, his lips very near her ear. "Sleepyhead, wake up…."

Jake watched Ana stir. She brought the hand that had been nestled between them upward, and rubbed her face in a haphazard motion, then sighed. Her hand fell back and nestled between them once again.

Smiling, Jake pressed a kiss to her hair, near her small, delicate ear. "Ana? It's Jake. It's time to wake up, sweetheart." This time, he settled his hand on her right shoulder and squeezed it enough to rouse her.

Ana stirred. She felt safe and loved. Warm and secure. The feel of a man's body against her own sang through her like lost music to her heart and soul. Wandering aimlessly in the realm of her colorful dream, she felt herself being embraced by a man, his body strong and capable against her more willowy one. Her nostrils flared and she dragged in his very male scent. It was like a lost perfume to her. Oh, it felt so good to be held once more! How she had missed having a man's body against hers, a man's arms around her. It was the most wonderful sensation in the world to Ana. For her, it signaled not only being loved, but being protected from the world of combat that raged around her daily. Being in the arms of Roberto had always made her feel safe in a world gone mad. Now that same feeling was back, even more strong and soothing than she'd ever experienced.

The voice, the deep, amused tone of a man, thrummed through her awakening senses. It wasn't Roberto's teasing voice. No, another's. Who? Her brows knitted. Ana stirred. The voice called to her again, and this time she felt a man's firm hand on her shoulder, squeezing her flesh just enough to bring her out of sleep's wings.

As she gradually woke, Ana became deliciously aware of her body pressed languidly against a man's hard, tall form. His arms were around her. Where her hand rested against his chest, she could feel the solid, steady beat of his heart. It was soothing. Wonderful. Best of all, as she nuzzled her cheek against his hard, muscled shoulder, she felt his fingertips trail lightly down her arm. Wild, hot tingles leaped wherever he stroked her. His touch was knowing, gentle and exploring. All those sensations made her body ache to complete herself with him. How she missed being whole with a man.

Trapped between sleep and wakefulness, Ana opened her palm and moved it up across his chest. Even though he wore clothes, she could feel the magnificence of his deeply muscled body. Making a soft sound, she barely opened her eyes and looked up…up into Jake's face, which was scant inches from her own. She blinked slowly several times, reorienting herself from her torrid dream state into the present.

The melodic song of a bird in the background reminded her she was in a small tent with Jake Travers on a hillside in Rainbow Valley. Her thoughts were sluggish, but her womanly instincts and primal needs were very active, bubbling just beneath the surface.

Jake's warming smile went straight to her heart like sunlight entering a darkened cavern where only grief had lived until this moment. Ana could not help herself as she slid her long, slender fingers up his chest, following the strong column of his neck until her palm came to rest on his sandpapery cheek. She saw his blue eyes grow stormy, his pupils huge and black as he studied her silently in the dawn light. Ana's breath snagged. Her heart thudded hard in her chest. He was going to kiss her. She saw it in his eyes, in the parting of his hard, male mouth. He was only inches away from her, his moist breath flowing across her face as he looked down at her. She saw a question in his eyes. Did she want him to kiss her? Ana could almost feel what he was thinking. Either that or she was very good at interpreting what she saw in his eyes.

Shaken, Ana slowly realized that Jake was lowering his guard. He was being vulnerable to her in a way that she'd never seen a man be with a woman. Warmth flowed through her, strong and nurturing. She felt his arm beneath her head curl, and his hand move to her shoulder to cup her and bring her upward just enough so that he could kiss her. Was that what she wanted? So much of her did. Ana became lost in the pale blue gaze that held hers. He was being gentle with her. He wanted her, but she also felt he wouldn't do anything unless she gave her approval.

She spread her fingers gently across his roughly stubbled cheek, then slid them up across his temple. His hair was short and silky to her sensitized fingers as she followed the curve of his skull. Lips parting, she lifted her chin and smiled softly up at Jake. Pulling his head downward, she pressed her lower body against his. Ana *wanted* to kiss him. She wanted to feel his mouth couple with hers. In one beautiful moment out of time, his mouth settled surely against her opening lips. How strong he felt, and yet, as Ana pressed her lips more insistently against his, she felt him controlling his reaction to her bold approach.

Smiling beneath his mouth, she moved her tongue across his flat lower lip. Instantly, his arms gripped her hard against him. A groan reverberated through him, like thunder rolling through Rainbow Valley. The sound resonated within her, and Ana's heart flew on wings of joy as she enjoyed the taste, the smell and feel of him as his mouth roughly took hers with command and sureness. Drowning in the onslaught, she curled herself fully against him to let him know how much she reveled in sharing this miraculous moment with him. Fire skittered down through the center of her body. The explosive flames that ignited deep within her made her moan as she felt his fingers slide sinuously through her hair.

Jake eased Ana onto her back, his fingers entangled in her silky, thick black hair, his body pressed urgently against hers. Her lips were full, soft and alluring. She tasted so sweet, so wanton as she returned his kiss with a boldness he'd never thought possible in a woman. As her hand ranged from his hair down his neck and across his back, he felt his control disintegrating. She was lush, hot, and just as eager to explore him as he was her. Yet a voice screamed at him that he couldn't take her like this. It wasn't right—for either of them. He wasn't the kind of man who had one-night stands. And although Ana intrigued him, and he hungered to know so much more about her, Jake knew making love to her at this moment wasn't the right thing to do. His conscience told him she was still grieving over Roberto. Was her response to him because of her loss? Jake wasn't sure. And if he wasn't sure, then he wanted to stop. If and when he made love to Ana, he wanted to know it was because she wanted him, not a ghost from her past.

Dragging his mouth away from hers, he looked down into her slumberous eyes. There were glints of gold within the cinnamon color there—the gold of desire. For him? How badly Jake wanted that to be so. Almost apologetically, he eased upward and took her into his arms and held her, just held her. Closing his eyes, he absorbed her very feminine body against his. Her dark hair swirled across his face and chest as she slid her arms around his neck, her brow pressed to his.

"You feel so damn good to me," he rasped, burying his face in her hair. "Beautiful, sweet, hot and good…"

His words vibrated through Ana. She hungrily absorbed them like a greedy beggar. Why had Jake broken their kiss? She had seen momentary regret in his eyes. Was he unsure of her? Ana didn't know. Easing out of his arms, she gave him a rueful smile and sat up. Running her fingers through her hair, she whispered, "I like the way you wake me up, Jake...." And she reached out and brushed his lower lip with her fingertips. Instantly, she saw his predatory eyes narrow upon her. Her body responded. She wanted to love him thoroughly and completely. But now was not the time, and Ana knew it. Jake had had the good sense to stop, even when she hadn't. Giving him a slightly embarrassed smile, Ana whispered unsteadily, "I don't regret it, Jake. None of it. It's been a long time since I've been awakened to a kiss. It was beautiful...."

Ana saw his eyes widen with surprise, and then she saw pleasure at her compliment. His mouth curved a little, much like a little boy's might as he was being rewarded. In that moment, Ana realized that regardless of what happened, Jake had opened to her and was remaining emotionally accessible to her. Tilting her head, she wrapped her arms around her knees, ensconced in the sleeping bag. "You are the most incredible man I've ever met. Did you know that?"

Jake warmed to her low, husky words. He saw the gold and cinnamon colors in her half-closed eyes, noticed that her hair was deliciously mussed. He fought the urge to pull her back into his arms and smooth out the tangles with his fingers. She invited that kind of intimacy. Smiling slightly, he murmured, "I don't understand. Did one kiss do it?"

Tilting her head back, Ana gave a low, melodic laugh. The dawn light was growing stronger, some of the shadows dissolving from his hardened features. Not having shaved, Jake looked highly dangerous, more animal than man to Ana. His primal qualities lurked just beneath the surface, and her womanly intuition reveled in that discovery.

"I like the way you kissed me." Ana gave him a wicked look. "You're open, Jake. Open to me. I've never seen a man able to lower his emotional guard like you did. It was wonderful. I loved it."

Loved it? Jake frowned. How was Ana using that word, *love?* Women frequently used the term, bandying it about in many ways, Jake had discovered long ago. What he felt for Ana, what was growing wildly and strongly in his heart, was overwhelming, but he was afraid to place a definitive word on it. The fear of losing a woman he loved was still too strong in him.

"It's easy to stay open around you, Ana," Jake declared.

She smiled more deeply. "Yes?"

He reached out and briefly squeezed her arm. "Yes. It's you. You're like this country. The more I learn of Peru, the more mystical and unexplained it becomes to me. You're like that."

"Ahh, yes, Peru's magic," she murmured. "You're right, no one is immune to it. When you come here, Peru wraps her arms around you like a long-lost lover, and you find yourself letting the world you knew slip away. You discover yourself wanting, needing to stay here with her instead. She's a very provocative lover, you know."

Grinning, Jake decided it was time to get up. If he

didn't, he was going to drag Ana back into his arms and love the hell out of her. "You and Peru are the same," he growled in warning, sitting up and rubbing his jaw. Ana looked gloriously disheveled, her red T-shirt rumpled, the dark green sleeping bag hiding the lower half of her body from him. She was so at one with nature. More like a wild animal, or even a beautiful butterfly, than a human being. When he told her that, her lips, soft and ripe, curved up wonderfully and made a sheet of heat flow through him. Her eyes smiled with such warmth toward him that Jake found himself becoming tongue-tied. Ana was not flirting with him. She was simply being herself. His heart tugged violently in his chest. He needed her in ways he didn't yet even begin to understand, and his longing drove him relentlessly. No woman had ever affected him like this. Ever.

Ana said, "I'll take that as a compliment." Looking at the watch on her wrist, she said, "Let's make breakfast and then break camp. We can be in Huayllabamba by noon. And then I can talk to the elder of the village and see what he knows about Tal."

Somberly, Jake unzipped his sleeping bag. Yes, Tal was the reason for him being here. The overwhelming reason. He tried to put his need for Ana on a back burner. "Do you think they'll tell you the truth?"

Ana slid out of her bag. "Oh, yes. The *campesinos* aren't given to lying. Especially to one of their own kind."

Jake stood beneath the hot sun in the middle of a recently furrowed field as he watched Ana approach a group of *campesinos* who sat in a circle not far away, being served lunch by their wives. The fifteen men were dressed in the traditional bright red leggings. Their mud-encrusted sandals were testament to their work. The women wore brightly colored hats and dresses as they poured a pink drink into the awaiting wooden cups of the men, who had toiled, probably since dawn, in this large field. Above them, the pale blue sky was patchy with cottony clouds. The valley was wide and surrounded by green hills clothed in trees and shrubs. Rainbow Valley was a wild and beautiful place.

Ana went over to the oldest man in the group and spoke in Quechua to him. Jake watched the old man's expression closely. The man was nearly toothless, his face long, lean and tobacco-brown, with hundreds of lines etched into it. Jake held his breath, hoping that they'd seen Tal and could give some sense of her whereabouts. This was the last village that she had gone to find water before she disappeared. Surely, the elder knew of her. Anxiety riffled through Jake as he saw several other *campesinos* speak excitedly to Ana when she knelt down to converse with them.

Impatient, Jake finally moved closer until he stood beside Ana. The talk had been going on for nearly five minutes and the discussion among the men was spirited. One of the women approached Jake and poured some of the pink drink into a cup and handed it to him. Jake took it and thanked her in Spanish. The older woman smiled and nodded deferentially to him. He held the cup, waiting.

Ana twisted to look up at Jake. "Good news. Tal

was here. She was staying with the elder leader here, Don Juan Hector. He said that last week a local drug lord, Rojas, came to his village. Rojas was trying to pressure Don Hector into ordering some of his younger men to carry bags of cocaine over the mountains for him. He refused Rojas's request. And then Rojas saw Tal. He asked Don Hector about her, and the elder told him she was here to help them sink a well so their children would stop dying. Rojas kidnapped Tal and told Hector that when he released ten of his younger men to him, he'd give Tal back to them.''

"Does Don Hector know where Rojas took Tal?'' Jake demanded darkly.

Ana stood. She turned and pointed toward a higher hill in the distance. "Yes. Rojas has a stronghold up there. It's a small villa that sits hidden under the jungle canopy. Juan is sure she's up there.''

"Have they seen Tal since Rojas took her?'' Jake's heart ached in fear.

"No, they haven't.''

"Is Rojas a killer?''

Ana shrugged. "The elder says Rojas is a bully. He's a braggart and he's loud and disrespectful to the elders here and at other villages. He has four goons as bodyguards, and they carry weapons on them at all times. Once, Rojas pistol-whipped Don Hector because he defied him.'' Ana frowned. "The old man doesn't hear well out of his left ear where Rojas hit him with the butt of his pistol. Other than that, no, Rojas isn't a killer.''

"Yet,'' Jake said quietly. Grimly, he looked back

at the *campesinos* and then at Ana. She was frowning, a worried look on her clean features as she studied the hill in the distance. "Do they know how to reach Rojas's place? Is there a path?" he asked.

Nodding, Ana said, "They're willing to show us a cow path that Rojas isn't aware of. It goes around the hill near Rojas's villa. There's also a road for car traffic, but we won't be able to use it for obvious reasons. Don Hector says they won't go any farther than that, Jake. They're afraid of Rojas. He's warned them that if anyone approaches the villa, he'll shoot to kill, so they leave him alone."

"What about Tal?"

Placing a comforting hand on his arm, Ana said, "I know you're upset, but these people are without arms, Jake. They aren't fighters. They're farmers. The elders are very upset at Tal being taken. Juan says she had quickly become like a daughter to him. He has prayed to the *apus* for help to get her out of Rojas's hands."

Grimly, Jake glared up at the hill in the distance. The day was hazy with humidity. The sun was beating down on him and sweat trickled down his temples. "I guess we're the answer to his prayers?"

She grinned a little. "You might say that. Listen, they want to feed us. I don't know about you, but I'm hungry after that hike up here. Let's sit with them. Their wives will serve us, and we'll find out the details about Rojas's villa. Then we can form a plan."

It was a wise decision. Still, Jake wanted to head straight to the villa and rescue Tal. He knew Ana's suggestion was the right one, however. As he sat down next to her, the *campesinos* all nodded in friendly fashion to him and spoke to him in Spanish instead of their native tongue, to make him feel a part of them. Jake managed a strained smile and nodded in return. Very soon, the women had given him a bowl heaped with steaming vegetables and a piece of beef. Huge hunks of thick, dark brown bread were pressed into his hand. He sat there in the middle of the field having lunch with the Quechua farmers.

Through the entire lunch, Ana spoke warmly and spiritedly with all the *campesinos* in their native tongue. Once the men had been served, the women sat with them and ate as well. Soon, some were laughing and pointing their fingers at Ana. Jake saw her blush deeply and avoid their sparkling eyes and wagging fingers.

"What are they saying to you?" he demanded, enjoying the sweet, grainy bread.

"Oh," Ana laughed as she chewed on an ear of boiled corn, "they're asking me about you."

"Oh?"

"Yes, they noticed I was wearing my *chalina*. The women said you looked very strong and would make a good husband in the fields for me. They want to know why I haven't taken my *chalina* off and wrapped it around your neck to let you know that I desired you."

Grinning wolfishly, Jake met the smiling, inquiring eyes of the Quechua farmers. Most of them were middle-aged, and when they grinned back at him he saw that most had teeth missing. Jake nodded and raised his brows, speaking to them in Spanish. "I think she'd make a good wife. Don't you?"

"Jake!"

The *campesinos* all howled with laughter and shook their heads vigorously. Several of them called to Ana in Quechua. Ana blushed even more deeply. The women cackled like old hens who had just laid eggs.

Ana gave him a dirty look. "Jake, they take things like that seriously here! You don't tease about such a thing! Now they'll all expect me to give you my *chalina.*"

Chuckling, he polished off the large piece of broiled beef and wiped his hands on the sides of his jeans. "Did I slip protocol?"

Giving him a dark look, Ana said, "You know you have."

The *campesinos* continued to tease Ana in Quechua. They motioned to the rainbow-colored scarf that hung around her neck. The women clucked indulgently and smiled hugely, motioning more than once toward Jake. One of the older women got up, waddled over and wrapped her thick brown fingers around Jake's upper arm, squeezing hard. She launched into a diatribe with Ana, motioning to his back and patting his spine.

"Oh, boy," Ana growled, "you've really set them off."

Jake smiled up at the older woman. She was nearly toothless, her smile touching her glinting black eyes. Her hands were very strong, but given the kind of life she had, Jake wasn't surprised. He gripped the woman's hand and patted it affectionately. She hid her eyes with her other hand and smiled girlishly before moving back to her husband's side.

"What'd I do?" Jake asked innocently. "Was she checking me out like a hunk of beefcake?"

Ana giggled, not immune to his sense of humor. "She was pointing out to me that you are not only well-built, but that you have a good, stout back. That indicates you'd make a fine farmer. She said I should be taken with you because you are young, strong and look very responsible. What else does a Quechua girl like me want?"

"Did she say I was handsome, too?"

"Don't push your luck, Travers."

Crowing, Jake slapped his hand on his thigh. All the *campesinos,* although they did not understand a word of English, seemed to know exactly what was being said, and laughed warmly.

Ana tried to keep the smile off her face. She saw the enjoyment and amusement in Jake's expression. He *was* terribly handsome, but there was no way she would let him know that. Especially now! The *campesinos* were acting like doting parents to her, telling her what a good catch Jake was. Her heart already knew that, and judging from the merriment in the elder's eyes, he also knew that she secretly liked Jake very much. Much more than she should.

"Let's get back to business, shall we?" Ana suggested archly. "Let's find out where the trail is, what the terrain's like, and then I'll call Captain Stevenson and let her know what's up."

Wiping the tears of laughter from his eyes, Jake grinned and said, "Fine, let's do it."

"You don't have to enjoy my discomfort so much, Jake Travers."

His teeth gleamed in the hot equatorial sunlight as he met and held her wide eyes, which were fraught with embarrassment. "Hey," he cajoled, "I meant it. You'd be a great partner. That was a compliment." More and more, Jake was coming to understand that though Ana called herself a warrior, she was a woman as well. And could be a mother. And a wife... He recalled that she wanted children someday. A husband. Family was as important to her as it was to him. Somehow, he had to reconcile that part of her that was a warrior with her very womanly nature. After this morning's kiss, he had begun to look at her differently. And his heart expanded wildly as his head made that hesitant admission.

Warmth stole into her heart. Ana could barely hold Jake's honest gaze. He meant what he'd said moments ago. It wasn't a joke even though he had said it in an offhand manner. Finishing her corn, she placed the cob back in the large wooden bowl and picked up the spoon to sup the delicious vegetable broth it had been cooked in. Ana wasn't ready to answer him. No, first they had to find Tal and get her to safety. Then she'd see how the wheel of fortune dealt with her in the next few days of her life....

Chapter Six

Jake sat next to an adobe hut with a thatched roof as Ana conversed on the iridium phone with Captain Maya Stevenson back at Black Jaguar base. He was stuffed from the heavy lunch that the *campesinos* had shared with them. Children sat around them, their dark brown faces and shining black eyes filled with curiosity about him. Many times they would shyly approach Jake, smiling softly, their hands extended to touch the white flesh of his arm.

No one could remain immune to these children, Jake decided, as he held out his hand and allowed six or seven of them to crowd around him to lightly touch and explore his skin. They spoke excitedly in Quechua, so he had no idea what they were saying. The looks of delight, awe and curiosity, though, were easy to read on their innocent faces. He kept on ear on Ana's conversation with Captain Stevenson as she spoke in rapid Spanish. As Ana stood out in the direct, hot sunlight, other children crowded around and gazed longingly up at her, their tiny brown hands extended and begging. She smiled and dug into one of her pockets as she talked.

Leaning over, Ana opened her hand, filled with colorfully wrapped hard candy. Instantly, the children dived for it, their small hands snatching pieces of it. Those that had surrounded Jake instantly left to see if they could get their share. Smiling down at them, Ana dug once more into her pocket. By the time she was done, all twelve children had a piece of hard candy in their mouths. Jake grinned up at her. Ana smiled back.

Instantly, his body tightened, because the curve of her lush lips reminded him of the tender, heated kiss they'd shared earlier that morning in their tent. The rainbow-colored *chalina* rested around her neck, the ends of the scarf dangling near her waist. She looked strong, capable and beautiful as she stood there, her eyes fastened on the hills above the village, where Rojas had his villa. Where Tal was.

Worried, Jake studied the rugged landscape. It wasn't going to be easy to get up there. The elder, Don Hector, had warned them that, beside the cow path, there was only one other route up to that villa, just wide enough for Rojas's cars and trucks to traverse.

Jake tried to suppress his fears over the fact that

Ana was going up there with him. His conscience ate at him.

Getting off the phone, Ana tucked it away in her knapsack. She moved to the side of the hut and stood beneath the roof, where there was some shade. The children gathered around them, sitting in the dirt, their brown feet bare.

Ana reached out and brought one little girl in a bright red-and-orange dress into her arms. She was barely four years old, her nose running. Digging into her pocket, Ana produced a tissue and sat the child on her knee to gently wipe her nose.

Jake smiled to himself. Ana would be a good mother, he could tell. The little girl, her hair shining and black, smiled adoringly up at her.

The child snuggled into Ana's arms, content to be held by her. Placing a kiss on the girl's hair, Ana turned and looked over at Jake. He had a strange, tender light burning in his eyes.

"What's that look for?" she demanded.

"Oh, nothing..."

"Jake?" She raised an eyebrow. A dull red flush crept into his cheeks. He looked endearing to her as he lowered his eyes and stared at the ground. When he did speak, it was a mumble.

"Just watching you with the kids... I thought you'd make a terrific mother, was all...." He tried to steel himself for her reaction. Ana probably didn't want to hear that kind of sexist remark from him, a man. When he lifted his head and forced himself to meet her gaze, he saw that she was giving him a tender look.

"You're a pushover with kids, too, Travers. They like to hang around you." She rocked the little girl in her arms. The child closed her eyes, content to be in Ana's arms.

For a moment, Jake fantasized that Ana was his wife and that was their little girl in her arms. The thought was shocking. Stunning. He had no idea where it had come from. Compressing his lips, he muttered, embarrassed, "They were just interested in this white-skinned *norteamericano.*"

Chuckling, Ana said as best she could with a straight face, "Oh, sure! Right..."

Moving uncomfortably, Jake said, "The kids are all so good-looking. Not an ugly dog in the bunch. I find that amazing."

"Jake!"

He gave her a nonplussed look. "What? What'd I say?"

Ana leaned against the wall, her arms around the little girl. "No child is ugly! Every mother thinks her baby is beautiful! It's a good thing these kids don't understand English. You could hurt their feelings."

Grimacing, he raised his eyes toward the sky, still peppered with soft white clouds. "Geez, Ana, you know what I mean. Not all babies are created equal. But these kids...they're all so beautiful...." He grasped for the right words, but they never came.

"Every mother thinks her baby is beautiful," Ana repeated, and gave him a dark look of censure.

Jake raised his hands in surrender. "Okay, okay..."

Several of the boys shyly approached Jake and sat

down around his feet, just to be near him. He had no candy to give the children. He had nothing except a pat on the shoulder or head, for each child. When he looked over at Ana, she had a pleased look on her face.

"You're really father material. I can always tell if a man's comfortable with children by whether he runs away from them or stays."

Jake smiled. Then, as he glanced at the hill once more, his thoughts moved to Tal. "You were talking to Captain Stevenson. What does she say about all of this? Can she help us or do we have to climb those hills to reach Rojas?" He took the dark blue baseball cap that he'd stuck in his pack and settled it on his head. Adjusting the bill so it came low to shade his eyes, he tried to squelch his worry for Tal.

"She said that the latest intel she just received on Rojas is that he's recently connected up with Faro Valentino, the drug lord we work so hard to try and stop over in our area."

"What does that mean to us?"

Frowning, Ana eased the little girl out of her arms and smoothed her bright red dress down around her spindly legs. "It means that if Rojas sees us, or knows we're coming for Tal, he could put in an emergency call to Valentino, and one of his Kamov Black Shark gunships would come our way."

Grimly, Jake said, "Ouch."

"Exactly. I don't want to be blown up by a rocket, either. And those Kamovs can find you under the best kind of tree cover. They have IR—infrared—and can see body heat no matter where we try to hide."

"We'll be dead ducks."

Her mouth crooked a little as she smoothed the child's black hair. "Must be *norteamericano* slang. We'll be dead, no matter what."

"Yeah, it's slang. But you got the bottom line right—a Kamov will hunt us down and kill us with no problem at all."

"Not to mention, the only thing we've got on us are two 9 mm Berettas," Ana said, smiling at the girl, who smiled shyly back at her. Directing her gaze to Jake, Ana added, "And using those pistols against the weaponry array on a Kamov would be like spitting at a fire-breathing dragon."

Jake nodded unhappily. "I'm struggling a lot with you going on this mission, Ana." He held up his hands. "Rightly or wrongly, I am." He saw her eyes darken. "It's...just...oh, hell...I worry that something will happen to you."

She pursed her lips. "Are you saying you don't trust me in this coming situation?"

Hanging his head, Jake nodded. "I trust you in a lot of ways, Ana, but yes, I have concerns."

"You're wondering if I can handle a pistol? If I can shoot to kill?" Her gaze was on his, a predatory look coming to her eyes.

Shrugging, Jake murmured, "Yes. I know *I* can. But can you? When the chips are down?"

"I'm able to pull the trigger when I'm in the Apache," she said slowly. The pain and worry in Jake's eyes touched her. Because she understood him better, his traditional leanings, Ana didn't take umbrage at his questioning of her. He was thinking out loud. At least he shared what was on his mind, when many men had real trouble communicating at all, so she felt hopeful about their dialogue. "Maybe we will assume this mission for different reasons, Jake. I'll be there for you. I'll guard your back. I'll tell you what I think. We'll work as a team, not separate from one another."

Sighing, he held her firm, unblinking gaze. Now he was seeing a little of the warrior side of her, the no-nonsense woman who was realistic and pragmatic about the situation. "I don't want you to get hurt. I don't want Tal hurt, either." He forced out the words, his voice filled with feeling.

"I don't want to see any of us hurt." Ana longed to reach out and touch Jake's arm, but now was not the time. "I'm going with you, Jake. That's the bottom line." She managed a slight, twisted smile meant to lighten the moment. "You're stuck with me."

He saw the way her lovely mouth flexed, and hotly recalled their wild, unexpected kiss earlier that morning. "You're a complex woman, Ana."

It was her turn to shrug her shoulders. Her smile increased. She saw hope burning in Jake's eyes. It was wonderful to know she could touch him with only a heartfelt smile. "And you're not complex?" She chuckled. "We'll get through this—together. You don't need to worry about me not being there for you. I won't leave you open to attack. I haven't lost a partner yet, and I'm sure not going to start by leaving you undefended."

Strong words from a strong woman, Jake decided. If a man had said those words, it would be plenty good enough to make him trust the guy. But the words were coming from a beautiful, feminine woman. Yet she was a warrior. Jake had to keep reminding himself of that. "Okay..." he murmured. "So, we're going to hump those hills to the villa?"

"Yes. If we get in trouble, I'm to call Maya on the iridium phone. She's going to keep an Apache on standby in case we need it pronto. But it would be a fifty-minute flight to get here, and that's a long time when you need firepower right away."

Nodding, Jake said, "Yeah. I can see we're really on our own." Studying Ana as she stood and brushed off the seat of her pants, his heart contracted with fear. Ana was too beautiful, too young to die. Jake didn't fear what they would be attempting to do; he was trained for it. Ana wasn't. He knew she wouldn't want to hear that from him. She might be an excellent helicopter pilot, but now she was a ground pounder, like him, and her wings were clipped.

"What if you stay here, in the village, Ana, and I go after my sister up there at that villa?"

"What?" Ana stared at him in shock. Jake's expression was dark and she saw worry in his eyes. "What are you muttering about? I won't stay here. You're going to need me up there."

Holding up his hand, he said, "Look, this is partly selfish when I say it, but I don't want you going in with me, Ana."

Ana stared down at him. The breeze was warm and humid as it moved through the village. Strands of her hair lifted momentarily around her shoulders. "Selfish?" Ana demanded pointedly.

Wiping his mouth with the back of his hand, Jake moved the little boys aside and carefully stood, not wanting to step on any of their small bare feet. "Yeah, selfish." He put his hands on his hips and studied the second hill topped with thick vegetation. Somewhere in the midst of all of it was the villa— the place where Tal was being held against her will. "I worry about you getting hurt, Ana. You're not a trained ground soldier like I am."

Ana came over and stood a few feet from him. "I should be angry but I'm not, Jake. I know where you're coming from."

She might understand part, Jake conceded, but not all of it. His heart burst with agony over the thought that Ana might get captured, raped or killed. None of those options were pleasant for him to think about. He shouldn't care about her, but he did. Plenty. How could that one soft, moist kiss shared so artlessly in the tent this morning have completely rearranged his head and heart? It blew him away. He was on unfamiliar ground. No woman had ever made him feel like this. Was this what they meant when they said a person was head over heels for someone? It must be, because all he could do was marvel at how his heart and body continually responded to Ana. Whether it was her smile, her eyes shining with such life or the way she touched that little girl's flyaway hair, something about Ana made him ache to possess her. He ached to have her in every way possible, not just sexually. A huge part of him wanted to delve deeply into her mind and heart, to hear about her thoughts, her ideas, her experiences of what life had taught her thus far. Ana left him feeling starved. He was like a gaunt wolf whose ribs were sticking out from going too long without a meal, then seeing one right in front of him: her.

Ana studied Jake in the silence. The bright sunlight only emphasized his expression. He was avoiding eye contact. Why? And then she was struck by the knowledge that maybe he was being protective of her. Because of their beautiful, shared kiss this morning? Ana tried not to dwell on that delicious moment too often. Every time Jake gave her that smoldering look, her gaze settled on that strong, curved male mouth of his and she felt herself going hot with a longing she'd never known before. Not even Roberto had affected her in this way. Not ever. Yet Jake could give her that boyish look, that cockeyed half smile, and she melted inwardly, her heart crying out for renewed contact with him.

"Look," Ana began haltingly, "let's keep our eye on the ball—Tal. She needs our help now, Jake. I— I..." She saw him lift his chin, his eyes narrowed upon her. Opening her hands, Ana whispered, "This is complicated."

"Us?"

Ana stared at him. So he was feeling the same way, about her, perhaps, as she was toward him? "Yes."

Jake sighed. It was time to be honest. "I don't want to see you hurt, Ana." He was afraid to tell her anything else but that. Seeing the tenderness in her large, expressive eyes, he felt his heart thud strongly in his chest. "I'm guilty of being a caveman, okay?" He held up his hand. "You're a woman. A beautiful woman. You're not like anyone I've ever met and I…well, I just don't want to see you hurt.'' Scowling, Jake held her thoughtful gaze. ''And where we're going, getting hurt is the least of several options that can happen to us. Killed is more like it.''

Ana moved toward him, her hand coming to rest on his arm. Feeling the strong muscles beneath her fingertips, she had the maddening urge to slide her hand upward in exploration. Censuring that urge, she gave him a slight, coaxing smile as he met her anxious gaze. ''Jake, you're very sweet, but really, I can take care of myself. I've been shot at so many times I've lost count. Once I had to crash-land the Apache because we took a hit by a Kamov. I've seen my share of life-and-death situations, all right?'' Her hand tightened briefly on his arm. ''Your sister is going to need both of us to spring her, if we can at all. I won't let you go up there alone. You don't know the territory. I do. That's why I'm along on this mission.''

Her hand was like a heated brand against his flesh. Jake squelched his desire to turn and simply lift his arms, place them around Ana's proud shoulders and pull her into his embrace. Looking at the colorful *chalina* she wore, he strongly reminded himself that Ana, if she were truly interested in him, would have taken off that scarf and placed it around *his* neck. And she hadn't. So maybe what he felt toward her was really one-sided.

Shrugging, Jake muttered, ''Okay, I hear you.''

''Good.'' Ana reluctantly removed her hand from his arm. ''We need to get going.'' She looked up, checking the position of the sun in the sky. ''This is a good time to leave. It's midafternoon. If we hike hard, we can reach the hill where the villa is located just before dark. Don Hector has told me where to find the old cattle trail that forks off from the main road up to the villa. He says that if we find it and follow it through the underbrush, there's a small *campesino* hut that we can stay in overnight. He said it's stocked with provisions, because they move their cows to a pasture on the other side of that hill in the summertime. We'd have food, a roof over our heads and be hidden from Rojas's men. What do you think?''

Jake liked the way Ana included him in the planning. She didn't have to, but like a good leader, she did, and that made him like her even more. Leaning down, he picked up her pack and held it out toward her so she could put her arms through it. ''Sounds like a plan to me. Let's go.''

Giving him a relieved look, Ana quickly shrugged on her pack and belted it up around her waist. She watched as Jake climbed into his own large knapsack. He resettled his baseball cap on his head to shade his eyes from the sunlight. The children surrounded them, calling to them and waving goodbye. Ana smiled and told them in Quechua that they'd return soon.

The trail leading out of the village and up the grassy slope of the first hill was wide enough for two people. Ana swung into stride with Jake, their hands occasionally brushing. Jake found his heart soaring with happiness even though the soldier in him, the wary ex-ranger, was fully operational. Just the brief touch of Ana's hand made him smile. Life was so funny, he decided. The chaotic, give-and-take of it left him feeling like a spinning top, unsure of what direction he was going. If someone had told him twenty-four hours ago he'd feel so strongly about a woman, he'd have laughed uproariously. Jake wasn't laughing now. All of a sudden, one kiss had shaken his well-ordered world, and he was in a spin, unsure of what direction was right.

"Look!" Ana whispered excitedly as she halted on the overgrown cattle trail, "I found the hut!" She pointed away from the barely visible path. Dusk was deepening and night was almost upon them. A soft rain was just beginning to fall.

Jake moved up and squinted into the thick underbrush beneath the spindly trees. He saw a dark shape a hundred feet off the path, although he had a helluva time trying to figure out what it was. Ana grinned triumphantly up at him and leaped off the path into the tangled brush, heading directly for it.

The hut was very small, Jake discovered. The *campesinos* had, according to Ana, hauled each adobe block up here to make it. He wasn't surprised that it was small, because those bricks weighed close to fifty pounds apiece. Ana hauled open the wooden door, which hung on leather hinges. She pulled out her flashlight and turned it on. Jake ducked inside the small doorway. The place smelled dank.

"This is nice," Ana said as she went to an old kerosene lamp in the corner. Kneeling down next to where the lamp sat on the hard-packed dirt floor, she took out waterproof matches from her pack and lit the lamp. Jake closed the door. The soft, falling rain could be barely heard on the thatched roof. The place was tiny; there was scarcely enough room for two people to stretch out and sleep.

As the lamplight filled the inner room, Jake shrugged out of his pack and placed it next to Ana's. He saw a small, rough-hewn table and two chairs in another corner. There was a large pile of dried grass to sleep on. Ana found a wooden box that had a huge rock on top of it, probably so no animal could get into it.

Jake leaned over. "Here, let me," he said, hefting the boulder and setting it down on the floor.

"Thanks," Ana said breathlessly. She flashed her light into the box. "Ohh, good—llama jerky. Great!" She pulled out the carefully wrapped dried meat. Looking up at Jake, she said, "Why don't you get out a couple of our MREs—Meals Ready to Eat? We'll supplement with this jerky. It will really fill us up and give us lots of protein for tomorrow's trek."

In no time they had spread their waterproof nylon sleeping bags together as a carpet to sit on as they enjoyed their meal. The rain increased, and in the distance, Ana could hear the thunder rolling and becoming stronger.

"I think it's going to storm for a while," she told him as she sipped the hot chicken soup he'd made for them.

In the dim light from the kerosene lamp, Jake thought the shadows did nothing but emphasize Ana's classic Indian facial structure. She ate with gusto and enjoyed every morsel of the meal he'd prepared for her. Ana wasn't like a lot of North American women, who picked at their food like birds in order to watch their weight. No, she enjoyed her food and ate a lot of it. But then, hiking at thirteen thousand feet would tend to burn off calories quickly in anyone.

"I'm glad the elder told us about this place," Jake said, looking up at the deep shadows of the roof above them. "I'd hate to be bedding down out there in that cold rain." At night, the temperature fell, sometimes to sixty degrees, even though it was jungle. When one was wet, sixty was very uncomfortable and cold.

"How's your headache? Did chewing the coca leaves make it go away?"

"Yes," Jake said, biting into the tough, dry llama jerky. He had had problems adjusting to the altitude, a nagging headache growing worse with each passing hour as they climbed higher and higher into the hill country. Ana had slipped him three dried leaves and told him to chew them and tuck them into his cheek. Within twenty minutes, his massive headache had disappeared.

"Good," Ana murmured. She sighed, smiled and put the rest of her MRE into another bag to carry in her pack. "What a wonderful meal!"

Grinning, Jake said, "Somehow, I think you're the kind of person who makes mud pies if she gets handed mud."

"I'm a born optimist, that's true." She lay on her side and propped her head up on her elbow. Jake was so very handsome in a primal way. She enjoyed watching him eat. He sat on his sleeping bag, legs crossed, his massive arms resting on his knees. Every time he met her gaze, she felt a thrill of joy flitter through her heart. His eyes told her so much, including how much he desired her. Ana seesawed between wanting Jake equally and freezing with fear at the thought. Could she risk reaching out and loving once again?

For a *campesino,* sexuality went hand in hand with the grave responsibility of liking and loving a partner. Sex for sex's sake wasn't supported in Peru; a couple must undertake a serious, long-term relationship with one another, not just a night in bed. Ana moved her fingers across the soft alpaca wool of her *chalina.* How many times today had she had the spontaneous desire to pull it off her neck and gently settle it around Jake's broad shoulders?

What would he do? Ana wondered. He knew now what the *chalina* meant. But he was from the north and she from the south. There was no way he would leave his country to stay here, with her. And Ana would never leave Peru, her family or friends to go north and live with Jake. Her spirit resided in Rainbow Valley. She'd been born of this land and had no desire to move away from her home. Still, in her heart of hearts, Ana fantasized about being in Jake's strong arms, and once more feeling his mouth hotly covering hers.

Ana's voice was soft. "So what about you? Have you ever thought of getting married?" She needed to know if their kiss was more than just danger and lust combined under the circumstances.

Wincing, Jake shook his head. "I was once…but not anymore…."

Hearing the pain in his voice, Ana sobered a little. "I'm sorry."

"It happened about two years ago," Jake managed to explain. "I was married…happily married…but I lost Carol in a car accident. There was an ice storm in South Carolina, where I was stationed. It was black ice, the kind you can't see until you're skidding out of control on it. Carol slammed into an oncoming truck." Quirking his mouth, Jake added hoarsely, "At least she died instantly."

Without thinking, Ana reached out and slid her fingers over his closed fist, which rested on his heavily muscled thigh. "I'm so sorry, Jake. So sorry." Looking at him through her thick black lashes, Ana saw the pain and grief still lingering in his eyes and the hard, suffering line of his mouth. "You and I share a common bond, then."

He frowned and tried to ignore the warmth, the tender touch of her fingers upon his closed fist. Jake made no move to touch her in return. If he did, it would be a helluva lot more than just clasping her fingers and giving them a polite squeeze in return. No, he wanted to turn around, put his arm around Ana's shoulders, draw her hotly against him and capture that soft, haunting mouth of hers. To drown in her womanly heat and earthy sensuality.

"Oh?" His voice was a croak. Why wouldn't she take her hand off his? Mentally, he was screaming at her to stop touching him. The heat in his loins was growing to a throbbing, unrelenting ache. Did Ana realize how she affected him? Probably not.

"As you know, I lost someone I loved with my life," Ana told him quietly, her eyes downcast. Just touching Jake, draping her fingers casually over his balled fist, helped her go on. Closing her eyes, Ana whispered, "It was a year ago that he was murdered by drug smugglers…and on some days, it seems like yesterday. Other days…" she lifted her head and managed a wobbly smile as Jake looked darkly down at her "…it seems like years ago. I guess it's the grief cycle." She touched her *chalina* gently and with reverence. "I decided that I have grieved long enough for what will never be, though he will always remain in my heart. By wearing my *chalina* once again, I am allowing my heart to move on, though. Life must be lived." Ana managed a broken smile. "Besides, I needed to wear this so the villagers will know me as onc of thcir own."

To hell with it, Jake decided, easing his hand open so that he could capture her smaller fingers in his. His need to console Ana overrode his mounting sexual hunger for her. Right now, from the look of devastation on her face, he knew he could comfort her, if only a little. "I don't know about you, but there're days when I feel like I'm cartwheeling completely out of control. I don't know where I'm going. I don't know who I am anymore. I'm looking…but I don't know for what. I just feel so damned lost…."

Without thinking, Ana squeezed his hand in return. She felt him stiffen and then relax. Slipping her fingers through his short, dark hair, she whispered, "To lose someone you love is to stand naked, without any protection, in our world. I'm so sorry you lost your wife, Jake. I can tell she was your life…."

Realizing Ana's reaction was one of compassion and not passion, Jake hungrily absorbed her touch, the feel of her fingers sliding gently across his sensitized flesh. Her lips were parted. She was so excruciatingly close. Jake wanted to kiss her once again. To drown in the soft fire of her mouth and lose himself within her in every possible way. But that wasn't right and he knew it. Ana was comforting him, nurturing him against his loss and pain. It wasn't a provocative or flirtatious gesture on her part, yet it made his loins ache like fire itself. No, she was comforting him and it felt damned good. How long had it been since he'd felt a woman's touch like hers? Carol had touched him in such a way, but the feeling was different. Somehow, Ana was able to move like fog through his wall of armor and simply reach in and hold his heart like a precious gift in her hands. She was a healer, he realized, just like her mother.

Easing away from her, Jake met her tear-filled eyes, which glimmered with sympathetic anguish and pain. How long had it been since someone cried for him? For his loss? Jake couldn't recall anyone doing that. Without thinking, he raised his other hand and, with his thumb, gently removed a tear that was trailing down her flushed cheek.

Yet his heart cringed in absolute terror of his desire. He couldn't fall for any woman again. He just couldn't. There was no way his heart could handle another loss like he'd had with Carol. No. Words jammed in his throat. He swallowed hard as he reluctantly removed his hand and released her.

"I hope Roberto knew what he had when you loved him," Jake managed to murmur in a strangled tone. She was like a rainbow in his hands—scintillating, mysterious. Soft, alluring and loving. Jake had never met a woman like her in his life.

"Yes, he knew...." Giving him a gentle smile, Ana sniffed. "I'm easily touched, as you can tell." She dug into her pocket for a tissue. The look on Jake's face, his naked need for her as a woman, made her tremble with desire. Desire that Ana had thought was destroyed a year ago. As she blotted her eyes, she began to realize that by reaching out and grazing her aching heart, Jake was bringing it back to life. Just as Inti, the sun god, would share his warming rays with newly planted seedlings to help them grow on the land she'd cultivated as a child growing up. Only this time, Ana was the seed that had remained frozen and cold, in the dark of grief for so long. Jake was her Inti. Her sun god. Just the heated look swimming in his narrowed blue eyes made her heart beat faster. Made her want to lean over and kiss the thinned line of his mouth, which revealed the pain and hurt he still carried deep within him.

Somehow, Ana knew she could heal him. But what was the risk to her? To her own freshly healed heart? Did she have the strength, the spirit, to reach out without regard for herself, ignore the cost to her emotionally, and do that for him? Ana was torn as never before. As she stuffed the tissue back into her pocket, she could not look up at Jake. She felt his sun-warm gaze upon her, but she didn't have the courage to meet and hold it, because if she did, she would be lost—forever. And right now, they had a mission to complete, a life to find and save. Their personal needs would have to be set aside.

Her heart protested her practical and unselfish decision, but Ana ignored it. At least for now...

She eased her hand from his and slowly rose. She opened up her sleeping bag and took off her boots, putting them to one side. She snuggled down into the sleeping bag, the dampness cooling to her. She heard Jake get up and move around. He was opening his sleeping bag and going to the other corner of the small hut. What she really wanted was Jake's warmth, his heart against hers as they slept in one another's arms. Closing her eyes, Ana knew the mission must come first. Tal must be found. There were no easy answers. Only questions with unacceptable answers. And one hard truth to swallow...

Tomorrow, they could die.

Later, after Jake had slid into his sleeping bag and turned out the kerosene lamp, Ana asked, "Do you think Rojas will have guards out around the villa?" The darkness in the hut was complete, their voices muted as they talked in low tones. He lay less than a foot away from her, and Ana wanted to reach out and touch him.

"I don't know. Rojas is supposed to be a two-bit player trying to learn how to be a drug lord," Jake said, turning on his back and staring up at the dark roof above them. He placed his hands behind his head, because if he didn't, he was going to brazenly reach out and drag Ana close beside him.

"Don Hector said Rojas has four men who carry guns and are always with him."

"Well," Jake sighed, closing his eyes, "tomorrow morning early, right at dawn, we'll make our move."

"If they've got dogs, we're in trouble."

"Yes. But Don Hector said Rojas didn't have any."

Ana snuggled down in her sleeping bag, lying on her side facing Jake. She couldn't see him in the darkness, for the hut had no windows. Above her, she could hear the soft plop, plop, plop of rain falling onto the thatched palm leaf roof. The thunder was coming closer, so she knew the storm was swinging their way. Jake sounded tired.

Compressing her lips, Ana curled her hands beneath the warm sleeping bag. How much she wanted to snuggle into Jake's arms and warm herself—and him—with their bodies tucked beside one another. Tomorrow, they could die. Her heart fluttered over that thought. And how was Tal? Had Rojas hurt her? Ana knew Jake thought the world of his sister; she saw it in his eyes every time he spoke of her, and of their life growing up together.

"If we find Tal tomorrow," Ana said softly, "we need to call Maya and get the Cobra helicopter in here to pick us all up."

"Yeah," Jake sighed. "I don't want to try and outrun Rojas and his guards. A life flight would be good."

Troubled, Ana asked, "What if Tal's hurt?"

"Then we'll do everything we can to help her." Jake tried to blot out the possibility of rape. A cold chill worked through him. "I'll be with her every step of the way, Ana. Morgan Trayhern said he'd help us, and I know he's in touch with your commanding officer. We'll get Tal whatever she needs."

"Even flying her out of the country and stateside?" Ana said the words haltingly, not really wanting to face the fact that tomorrow, Jake could be gone. Forever. How much Ana wanted to love him! To kiss him, to lose herself in his strong, tender arms and mouth. A bittersweet feeling flooded her aching heart. Ana knew better. She was chasing a dream. Once Jake rescued his sister, he would be gone for good.

"I'll do whatever we have to, Ana." Hearing the concern and trepidation in her tone, Jake wanted to add, *And I want you at my side—always....* But he didn't say those words. He knew Ana would never leave Peru. Not for him, not for anything or anyone. It felt as if someone were drilling a hole directly into his heart, the way the pain radiated throughout his chest. In an effort to avoid it, he asked, "And what will you do after we get Tal to safety?"

Closing her eyes, Ana said, "Go back to the base. I'm needed. The pilots have been flying shorthanded without me." For once, she wished she could just go off spontaneously with Jake. "Why?"

Groaning, Jake shut his eyes. Could he risk it all and say what lay in his heart? "I just wondered, is all. I know you have responsibilities, too." She would make a wonderful mother. The way she'd held the children of the village, the way they adored her...yes,

Ana was all those things he'd looked for in a woman. As a wife and partner for life. Still, he knew she was a warrior whose heart was with her mission in Peru, though he struggled to accept her in this role. He didn't know many women who had a passion for combat. But then, didn't he have the same passion? Why couldn't he get over his prejudice?

Hearing the wistful tone in his voice, Ana rubbed her face and allowed his deep voice to soothe her raw emotions and needs. "I know…we all have responsibilities," she whispered. Heart thudding in her breast, Ana realized she could not leave Maya and her sister pilots in the lurch just to be with Jake.

"Get some sleep, Ana. Tomorrow is going to come too soon, anyway…."

Chapter Seven

Ana's heart pounded hard in her chest as they lay on a bush-covered slope just below Rojas's villa. Wisps of fog came and went around the top of the mountain where the villa sat. From their vantage point, they could not be seen. Keeping her mouth open so her breathing couldn't be heard, Ana scrunched her body tightly against Jake's. She felt the dampness of the vegetation soaking into her jacket as she lay on her stomach. Jake peered cautiously over the bank and looked for guards. It was barely 9:00 a.m. and no one was stirring. They had been hiking since dawn on the cow path that led up the hillside toward the rear of the villa.

She watched as Jake silently scanned the grassy yard. Off to one side, the bulk of the hilltop had been bulldozed away and there was a round slab of concrete. He had no doubt that it was a helicopter landing pad. The villa was a one-story, dark gray adobe structure with a red, Spanish tile roof. Nothing fancy. Rojas was a drug lord in the making and he couldn't yet afford the luxurious, two- or three-story villas such as Faro Valentino had.

Ana remained unmoving and let Jake do what he did best as a ranger. Her arms were scratched from making her way up the vine-choked cow path, badly overgrown during the season it was not in use. Her fingers were scraped and chilled. Both she and Jake were muddy from their climb. Jake had his gun drawn, as did she. They had silencers in place.

Jake eased back down and turned his head toward Ana's. Keeping his voice low, he said, "I don't see anything." He saw the worry banked in her eyes as he gazed at her. This morning, she had fashioned her hair into two thick, long braids to keep it out of the way. The *chalina* was around her neck, but tucked beneath her jacket, barely visible. The colors against her golden flesh looked beautiful. Jake quenched his urge to kiss her.

"Let me go to the house," Ana whispered in a low voice.

His eyes flared with surprise. Jake saw the resolve in them. "No way, Ana!" His voice was intense and didn't brook argument. "*You* stay here. I'll go. There's a door just across the yard, no more than fifty feet away. You stay here and keep watch."

Frantically, Ana looked at him. She absorbed his

weight and warmth beside her. "Jake, that's dangerous! You don't know the layout of this villa!"

"And you don't, either. We can't wait all day hoping to see Tal. What if she's hurt?"

Ana saw the raw anguish in Jake's eyes. Reaching out, she gripped his hand, her muddy fingers curving strongly about his. "I know...I know. I just wish there was a better—safer—plan...."

Just then, Ana heard a sound. And it sent a chill crawling up her spine. Her fingers tightened on Jake's. "Listen," she whispered, frantically searching the foggy mist that hung like a heavy blanket around the top of the hill.

He cursed softly. "A helicopter..."

"A Kamov."

His eyes narrowed on Ana's taut expression. Blood was draining from her face.

"Damn!" He remained hunkered down. Kamovs could fly in dense fog and clouds because they had the instruments to negotiate such nasty weather conditions without crashing. Just then, he heard a door in the villa open. Male voices drifted their way. Easing up slightly, Jake spotted two military-garbed guards with weapons and another, shorter man in the middle. The shorter man was dressed in an expensive set of slacks, dark brown Italian shoes and a white silk shirt. It was Rojas. Feeling Ana's hand gripping his arm, Jake slid back down.

"Rojas. Two guards with him..."

"Don't move!" she rasped. Ana looked upward. The thudding rotors were approaching, making the entire hilltop and everything on it, including the trees, tremble.

"What if they're taking Tal away in it?"

Ana shook her head. "The Kamov is a one-seater, Jake. No, it's probably a pilot landing to pick up some cocaine and ferry it to Bolivia. Just sit tight. Please…"

Her eyes begged him to stay where he was. Jake was torn. He saw Rojas and his two men move around the house toward the concrete landing pad on the other side of the villa. The door was ajar. It was a perfect opportunity.

Gripping Ana by the shoulder, he said, "I'm going in. There isn't going to be a better time. They're engaged in that Kamov landing and the transfer of coke." He saw her eyes widen in fear—for him. Her lips parted. Giving her a tight smile, Jake leaned over and crushed his mouth against hers.

Ana's cry of fear was drowned in her throat as his mouth moved commandingly across her lips. His breath was warm and moist, his hand strong and guiding against the back of her head as he drank swiftly of her.

Heat and lights exploded behind her closed eyelids. Urgently, Ana returned his unexpected kiss. Just as she leaned forward, her hand on his arm, he tore his mouth from hers. The dark, predatory gleam in his narrowed eyes made her want to sob. This was a part of Jake she hadn't seen before. The warrior. The lethal hunter.

"Wait for me?" he rasped.

Nodding and unable to speak, Ana touched her

throbbing lips where he'd imprinted his maleness upon her.

Digging the toes of his muddy boots into the soft surface, Jake lunged upward. The Kamov's double rotors were shaking the hell out of the hill now. The noise would more than cover his movements. He still couldn't see the helicopter through the thick fog that hung just above the villa. Sprinting for the back door, Jake made it inside. Instantly, he held the pistol up in both hands, his back pressed to the wall. Breathing hard, he jerked a look down the hallway. It was empty. Taking a quick glance around, Jake saw two doors standing open. Halfway down the hall on the right was a third door. It was shut. Was Tal in there? He followed his hunch.

Tiptoeing down the carpeted expanse, Jake reached the door. There was no sign of a bolt or padlock. He saw that the button in the center of the doorknob was pressed inward, indicating it had been locked from this side. Quickly slipping his hand forward, he jiggled the knob. It didn't budge. He pressed the button and it popped out.

Taking a breath, Jake jerked the door open and moved swiftly into the room.

"Tal!"

His sister was standing at a window with bars across it. She turned. Her oval face went pale. "Jake!" His name tore from her lips. Tal's blue eyes widened in shock at his unexpected appearance.

"Shh!" Jake quickly shut the door and holstered his pistol. He turned. Tal was five feet nine inches tall. She wore her thick blond hair in a pixie-style cut.

Uttering his name again, Tal threw her arms around his shoulders, pressed her face against his shoulder and sobbed.

"Oh, Jake! How did you get here?"

He held her tightly for just a moment. Then, placing his hands on his sister's shoulders, he searched her tearful features. Tal had a black eye, and he saw old, dried blood at one corner of her mouth, the flesh puffy along her right cheek and nose.

"Tal, you're hurt...who did this to you?"

She wrinkled her nose and stared up at him. "It's nothing. I'm okay." Her voice trembled. Tears came to her eyes. "I thought I was a gonner, Jake. How...I mean...I never thought *you* would be here." She gave him a giddy, almost hysterical laugh of relief, her blue eyes sparkling with hope.

Outside, Jake could hear the Kamov landing. The entire villa shook from the powerful buffeting of the rotors. Gripping her by the arm, he looked around. Tal was dressed in her usual type of clothes—a short-sleeved white blouse, jeans and hiking boots.

"We've gotta get out of here, Tal. We've only got a minute or so. Where's your jacket?"

She quickly moved to the bed and grabbed a dark green nylon jacket from the foot of it. "Here. Let's go!"

Nodding, Jake pulled out his pistol, and with his other arm, kept Tal behind him. "First we gotta get out into the hall. How many guards?"

"Four."

Damn. Two were with Rojas. Where were the other two? Possibly waiting at the landing pad with the cocaine? Jake hoped so. Easing the door open, he quickly looked up and down the hall. It was empty. Swinging the door wide, he said in a gruff tone, "Run to the end of the hall by the door. *Don't* go outside yet. Wait for me."

Nodding and wiping her cheeks free of tears, Tal quickly slipped past him.

Turning, Jake made sure the door was shut and the button pressed in. That way, Rojas and his guards would think that Tal was still locked away in the room. Unless they went to check on her, no one would realize she was gone. And that bought them time. Time they desperately needed.

Running down the hall as quietly as possible, Jake saw his sister waiting tensely at the door. Her face was pale. His gut told him something terrible had happened to Tal. It made him nauseous to think what might have. Her blond hair was unkempt, and she had dark purple circles beneath her glorious blue eyes. Tal was such an outgoing person, a risk taker, a real extrovert who loved life and people. She was always trying to help others less fortunate than her. As he ran toward her, it sickened Jake to realize that she'd been injured. When he reached Tal, he quickly searched her features. Jake knew now that she'd been beaten—often. Her once fine, thin nose had a bump on it. Swelling was still there from someone hitting her hard and breaking it. Rage swelled up in him. He wanted to kill the bastard who had touched Tal. She didn't deserve this. None of it.

Controlling his fury, Jake carefully eased the back door open. Tal hovered at his back, her hand resting tentatively on his shoulder as she waited for him to tell her what to do. Jerking his head in both directions, Jake searched for Ana. He saw her crouched at the lip of the embankment. Ana made a sharp gesture for them to make a run for it.

"Come on!" he rasped, grabbing Tal's hand and pulling her out of the doorway. The Kamov had just landed. Wind was whirling around the hilltop like a tornado. The thumping sounds of the blades were ear shattering, the high whine of the engines on the Russian-made helicopter nearly a shriek.

"See that woman?" Jake said in Tal's ear, and motioned toward Ana.

"Y-yes. A friend?"

"Yes. Ana Cortina is her name. Run to her, Tal. Do as she tells you."

Tal didn't hesitate. She covered the fifty feet to the embankment in a hurry, leaped down it and disappeared. So did Ana.

Jake's heart was pounding. He held the pistol ready and once more checked both directions as he eased out of the door and shut it quietly behind him. *Now!*

Digging his feet into the muddy lawn, Jake sprinted for the cover of the bank. Ana was hunkered down there, her pistol drawn, her eyes narrow as she swept the area with her gaze as he ran toward her.

With a grunt, Jake leaped forward, flying through the air. Landing with a thud, he rolled once and slammed into some brush. Safe! They were safe! Instantly on his feet, he saw Tal crouched down, watching them with wide eyes. Looking to his left, he watched as Ana slid unceremoniously down the muddy bank. She holstered her pistol and offered her hand to Tal.

"Tal, I'm Lieutenant Ana Cortina. I'm helping Jake on this mission. Are you okay?"

With a wobbly grin, Tal took Ana's proffered hand and got to her feet. "Yeah, I want to run like the dickens. Can we get out of here? It's been a nightmare...." She looked up as Jake approached.

Ana saw all the lumps and swelling on Tal's face. She looked over and saw the rage burning in Jake's eyes. Tal had been badly beaten a number of times, Ana realized.

"Jake, I've called in help," Ana said as he went over to his sister and gave her a quick hug.

Nodding, Jake turned and asked, "What's their ETA—estimated time of arrival?"

Ana moved past them. They had to get back to the cattle trail and start out of here, pronto. "Maya is sending the Cobra to pick us up down below. She's also sending an Apache to take on the Kamov, if necessary."

"What's their ETA?" he repeated.

Ana grimaced. "Forty-five minutes. We've got to get down off this hill by then. Can we do it?" It had taken them nearly three hours to climb the hill. Of course, going down was easier, and they had marked the path accordingly, so some speed could be made. Still, Ana looked unhappily at all the underbrush and the thick, gnarled roots that stuck up everywhere in the damp, moist ground. Those roots that would snag their feet and make them trip and fall.

Jake gripped his sister's smaller hand and tugged

her along with him. "We're going to try. Tal, can you push hard?" He found the trail and they moved quickly through the brush.

Nodding her head, Tal whispered, "I'll do *anything* to get out of here, Jake. Just show me the way."

Ana brought up the rear. Her job was to make sure that Rojas or his guards didn't come after them. And if they did, she would have to stop them. At all costs, Tal was to be gotten to safety. Ana's heart ached for the woman. Tal was very pretty and looked a lot like Jake. There was no mistaking the love between them, and Ana smiled to herself. Tal was worth risking their lives for. Ana placed her hand on the iridium phone in her waist belt, knowing she'd have to continue to keep Captain Stevenson, who was piloting the Apache, apprised of their ever-changing situation.

Heart pounding, Ana hurried to catch up. Jake and Tal were flying through the underbrush like two deer. It was a good thing Tal was athletic and in excellent shape, Ana thought. The hill was steep, and descending it required fluidity and flexibility. If a vine caught the toe of one of their boots, they could go flying and possibly break an ankle or worse in the fall.

Tal was gasping for breath as they reached the halfway mark down the hill. Jake caught her before she fell. Ana hurried toward them. It had taken them twenty-five minutes to reach this point. Holding his sister under his arm, Jake rasped, "Tal, you okay? How are you holding up?"

Tal groaned and wrapped her arm around Jake's narrow waist as she pointed, her mouth open. Then she leaned over and tried to catch her breath.

Ana ran up to them, her eyes worried as she pinned Jake with her gaze.

"The Kamov..." she warned, looking back up the hill. The fog was beginning to dissipate as the sun rose higher in the sky. Soon, Ana knew, it would be clear enough to see the entire crown of the hill, and below it, Rainbow Valley. Although they were well hidden beneath the cover of the trees, Ana knew the Kamov would be able to "see" them with its infrared equipment. They were not safe.

"What about it?" Jake demanded, breathing hard. The helicopter was still on the apron, the rotors turning at a much slower speed than before.

Worriedly, Ana said, "If they find out Tal's gone, they'll send the Kamov up after us. They'll use IR— infrared—and locate us."

Jake nodded. "Then let's hope they don't check to see if Tal's in her room or not." He glanced down at his sister. Her face was pale. Perspiration dotted her gleaming flesh, accentuating all the bruises and swelling. He wanted to kill whoever had done this to her.

Ana looked at her watch. "Go on. I'm going to check in with Captain Stevenson via the iridium phone and see if they're on schedule. I'll catch up with you in a minute."

Jake nailed Ana with a dark look. "Be careful."

Giving him a slight smile, Ana pulled the phone from her belt. "Always."

"Come on, Tal," Jake coaxed, taking his sister's hand in his and leading her down the hill on the barely visible trail.

"Black Jaguar One, this is Black Jaguar Three.

Over.'' Ana hunkered down in the brush, one knee pressed to the rich, damp earth, the satellite phone against her ear. She waited impatiently for the satellite link to establish.

''Black Jaguar Three, this is One. What's your situation? Over.''

The reassuring, husky voice of her commanding officer made Ana feel a tad better. The link was scratchy. In the mountains, it always was. ''We've got the package. We're halfway down the hill. We should reach the base in twenty minutes. What's your ETA? Over.''

''Black Jaguar Three, that's good news. We'll reach you in twenty minutes. Over.''

''Roger. There's an old ravine at the base. The only time it has water in it is during the spring flood. There's enough room in it to land the Cobra. Do you have the ravine marked on your map? Over.'' Ana knew that the days and weeks they had spent painstakingly mapping all the nooks and crannies of the region would pay off now. She waited for a response, sure that Maya's copilot was looking the terrain over on her HUD—heads up display—in the cockpit. All the knowledge of terrain they'd amassed over the years was fed into the computer software aboard the Apache for quick access at times like this.

''Black Jaguar Three, that's a roger. We've got the ravine buttonholed. There's one spot where the ravine opens out into a plain. That's where you want us to land? Over.''

Grinning, Ana said, ''Roger that, Black Jaguar One.'' She heard a sound that sent fear rippling through her. "Hold on…" she told Captain Stevenson. Lifting her head, Ana heard shouts. Men were yelling. They were angry. In a flash, Ana realized what they were upset about: they'd found that Tal was missing.

Ana's heart thudded in her chest. Coldness shot through her. "Black Jaguar One, they've found the package missing. That means the Black Shark will take to the air and start a search with IR for us. We're going to be hunted down. Over."

"Roger. We're redlining it right now. Our ETA will be…ten minutes. Try to hang on…."

Throat constricting, Ana whispered, "Roger. Black Jaguar Three out." With shaking hands, she rose and placed the iridium phone back into her belt. She heard the Kamov's engines begin to shriek. It was getting ready for takeoff speed—to hunt them down.

Wheeling around, Ana took off at a sprint. She leaped over small bushes, twisted around larger ones and dodged the ever-present trees that grew thickly along the cow path. She couldn't see Jake yet. Breath tore from her. Her lungs felt on fire as she pushed herself to full speed, hurtling down the hill. She must tell Jake what had happened.

Jake heard the crashing of underbrush behind him. Friend or enemy? He wasn't sure. It should be Ana, but he couldn't take the risk. Halting Tal, he placed her behind a tree.

"Wait there," he ordered heavily. He pulled out his pistol and moved rapidly toward the sound. Jake heard the Kamov powering up. Had it gotten the cocaine, and was it now flying toward Bolivia? He hoped so. Jogging up the path a short way, he saw Ana running full speed down it. Her face was tense. He saw fear in her expression as she bobbed and leaped, running toward him at full speed.

Holding his hand out, he caught her as she nearly crashed into him. She gripped him, sobbing for breath.

"They know Tal's missing!" Ana sobbed. She stood up, her knees wobbly with fear. "The Kamov is coming after us!"

"Damn!" Jake rasped. He released Ana and looked up toward the patchy blue sky above the trees. "Have you contacted Captain Stevenson?"

Leaning over, her hands on her knees, head bowed, Ana gasped, "Yes...her ETA...is ten minutes. They're trying to get here...to save us. I don't know..." Ana straightened. Jake's eyes were wide with understanding. "I don't know if they'll be here in time.... We're as good as dead...."

"Then we need to split up," Jake ordered, breathing in gulps. "I'll stay here, you take Tal down to where you're going to meet the Cobra." He gripped Ana's arm when he saw protest in her eyes. "There's no time to argue about this, dammit. Just go, Ana. Take Tal with you. *Now*."

"No...Jake...."

He gripped her to him, their faces inches apart. "Listen to me, Ana. You get my sister out of here. Make sure she's safe. Do you understand?" His gaze dug mercilessly into her wide eyes. Her lips parted. How badly he wanted to kiss her one more time. Maybe the last time.

Ana pulled out of his grip. Quickly, she took off her *chalina* and threw it around his neck, tying it so it wouldn't fall off. The ends trailed across his chest. "You come back to me, Jake Travers," she whispered fiercely, her eyes brimming with tears. "You hear me? Do you?" Her voice cracked with pain, with terror. They'd be lucky if any of them survived the minutes ahead.

Stunned, Jake felt the soft alpaca wool of the scarf against his hot, sweaty neck. He saw love and fear in Ana's huge, widening eyes. His heart soared with joy. With anguish. No one knew better than they did what the Kamov was capable of doing to them in very short order. He lifted one end of the scarf in his muddy fist.

"Okay...okay, Ana...just get out of here. Stay *safe*. I'll try and get the Kamov to come after me. Just get Tal outta here...." He gulped and held Ana's damp eyes. "I love you—you know that, don't you?" There, he'd said it.

The Kamov was taking off. The entire hillside trembled with the power of the hunter aircraft lifting into the sky.

Choking, Ana whispered, "And I love you, too, Jake...." She reached out and gripped his hand. "I want the time...the time to get to know you—"

"Get outta here!" he ordered hoarsely. "Run! *Now!*"

There was no time left. Ana felt him grip her fingers one last time and then release her. Turning, the landscape blurry through her tears, Ana ran down the hill to where Tal was standing. Sobbing, Ana tried to gather in her powerful emotions. The Kamov would hunt them down with the cold precision of a lethal hunter. Jake was putting his life on the line in drawing the Kamov away from them.

Reaching out, Ana grabbed Tal's hand. "Come on, we've got ten minutes to make that ravine where the helicopter is coming in to rescue us!"

Tal hesitated. "But Jake—"

"No time, Tal! Come on, follow me! The Kamov's up and is going to hunt us. Rojas knows you've escaped. Hurry!"

Tal jerkily turned away from Jake and swiftly followed Ana as she headed on down the trail. Above them, she could hear the thump, thump, thump of the Kamov moving slowly toward them. Gasping for breath, Tal pushed herself. Her brother was nowhere near them.

With superhuman effort, Tal managed to come abreast of Ana. "Where's Jake?" she cried.

Ana shook her head. "He's going to try and lure the Kamov off to hunt him and not us. Keep running!"

"But," Tal cried, "can't we help him?"

"No!" Ana reached out and grabbed Tal's arm as she started to slow down. "Nothing can stop a Kamov except an Apache helicopter. We've got one coming, Tal. It's a question of time." Ana jerked Tal's arm and pushed the woman ahead of her. "Keep running! We've got to make that rendezvous point at the base of the hill."

"But Jake!" Tal cried.

Ana saw tears streaking down Tal's face. She

wanted to sob herself. Tal knew what Jake was doing: making himself a target so that they might survive.

Maybe they had a chance. Ana knew that the Kamov pilot had to not only fly the machine but work the weapons and radar simultaneously. That took time. The Apaches had two pilots—one to fly, the other to work the instruments, weapons and radar. In the long run, the Apache was quicker on the draw because of it. The Kamov pilot might be over-whelmed with multiple demands on his attention. That might play in their favor as seconds and minutes of precious time slipped by. Ana hoped that would be the case.

"Keep running!" Ana barked. "Run for your life!" She shoved Tal hard to force her to run faster, drawing her pistol as she followed. Ana knew their headlong dash for the ravine was going to be close. If the Kamov swept his IR toward them and not Jake, *they* could become his target. No, nothing was guaranteed now, and Ana knew it. Keeping her ears tuned to the approaching Kamov, she felt her heart bleed with fear and joy. Jake had said he loved her! And she'd blurted out her love for him as well.

How had it happened? When? Ana wasn't sure at all. As she jumped over some roots, she saw Tal's boot snag on a vine. Jake's sister went tumbling end over end and landed in a heap against a tree trunk. Sobbing for breath, Ana skidded to a halt, mud flying in all directions. Curving her hand around Tal's arm, she helped her stand. The front of Tal's clothing was nothing but mud. Her hair was sprayed with it from her fall.

"You okay?" Ana gasped, keeping a hand on her arm.

"Yeah, yeah, I'm okay."

Gasping, Ana ordered, "Then keep running. Concentrate, Tal. Watch where you're putting your feet!"

Tal wiped her shaking fingers through her stringy blond hair. Glancing back up the trail, where she knew Jake was, she turned and started to run once again.

Ana's heart beat hard in her chest. She had to make sure Tal got to the landing area. As much as she wanted to go to Jake, Ana knew she couldn't. He was alone. He was going to take on one of the world's most lethal hunter helicopters, and she knew he couldn't possibly win the confrontation. Could he?

Chapter Eight

Jake found a small gap, not large enough to be called a clearing, between the trees so that he could take a clean shot at the approaching Kamov. The helicopter was moving slowly, and as Jake pressed himself against a tree to steady his aim, he could feel the puncturing vibration of the double rotors on the gunship as it crawled toward him.

Sweat ran down into his eyes. He lifted his arms, both hands wrapped around the butt of the pistol. He pressed his left wrist against the tree, the barrel pointing upward. Would the Kamov's IR detect his body heat behind this tree? Jake wasn't sure. He knew the infrared equipment was powerful and could penetrate thick tree core at a distance, but how much, exactly, he wasn't sure. The wind began to whip and change direction. Twigs, leaves and small branches began to break and fly around him like a battering tornado as the Kamov inched closer.

Blinking his eyes, his breathing harsh and ragged, Jake jerked a look over his shoulder. He couldn't see Ana or Tal. They must be down at the base of the hill by now. Safe in the ravine awaiting rescue by the Cobra. Where was that damned Kamov? The entire jungle began to vibrate around him. The power of the gunship was terrifying, and Jake had never had to experience the Russian helicopter in such a situation. Every leaf trembled. Bushes swayed violently as if in an earth tremor. Birds shot past him. He saw several small mammals running ahead of the creeping Kamov, terrified by the thunderous sound and ear-splitting vibration.

Jake knew the Kamov had a 30 mm cannon, with shells as big as a man's fist, which it could spit out at him like a Gatling gun. Or would the pilot use a rocket, which would blow up a helluva lot of real estate in the process and him along with it? Digging his right boot into the mud, Jake tried to anchor himself and wait. Waiting was the hardest part. He would have only a few seconds to try and place one of the nine bullets in his pistol into the rotor assembly cuff at the top of the gunship. The rotor assembly was the most vulnerable part on any helicopter. Had the Russians protected it with a thin titanium wall to deflect bullets? Again, Jake didn't know.

Were the cockpit windows bulletproof like they were in an Apache's windshield? Jake thought about trying to kill the pilot instead of trying for that one lucky shot into the assembly cuff. An Apache cockpit could withstand a direct hit from a 30 mm cannon and not shatter. If the Kamov was similarly designed, then his measly 9 mm bullets would bounce off that cockpit window like flies trying to kill a gorilla.

The ground began to tremble beneath his booted feet. The Kamov was coming....

Jake held his breath. He aimed the pistol skyward, his arm steady against the trunk of the tree. He saw the tips of the double rotors along with the ski-shaped snout on the Black Shark appear in the clearing. It was a lethal-looking machine. It stopped its forward progress. It was hunting...for him.

Jake released an explosive breath. The Kamov was barely six feet above the top of the jungle canopy. He saw the pilot clearly; he was in a flak vest and helmet, a dark visor drawn down across the upper half of his grim-looking face. Jake watched, almost mesmerized, as the pilot looked at his instruments—to get a fix on him. The Kamov needed to come just a few feet closer in order for Jake to take the shot at the rotor cuff.

Come on! Come on, you bastard! Just a few more feet...

Jake stopped breathing. The Kamov moved cautiously forward. It hovered again. The ground shook and shuddered around him. Wind whipped through the jungle and stung his eyes. Dirt and debris whirled everywhere. Jake was unable to protect his eyes and blinked rapidly in order to keep a bead on the Kamov at the same time. His hands gripped the pistol hard. Slowly, his finger brushed the trigger. The pistol bucked sharply. The sound of it firing was drowned out by the roar of the Kamov's powerful engines.

Jake saw a spark of light explode near the cuff. He squinted. The rotor cuff had protection around it. *Damn!* The pilot seemed oblivious to him having fired off a shot. Mouth tightening, Jake swung the pistol and aimed it directly at the pilot. The Kamov's tail moved slightly, as if to line up directly with where Jake was hiding, until the entire front of the cockpit, with its lethal rockets, was aimed at him.

Jake fired three bullets in rapid succession. He watched in disbelief as they all struck the front window and deflected. This time the pilot reacted. He probably heard the bullets cracking into the hardened Plexiglas surface.

Digging his boots into the damp soil, Jake took off. He knew the Kamov had him on IR. If he didn't move, he was dead. Heading in the opposite direction from the ravine at the base of the hill, Jake ran as hard as he could.

He heard the pitch and whine on the Kamov's engines change. Jerking a look up through the thick trees, he saw the Black Shark slowly move—toward him. His heart pounded savagely in his chest as he hit the cow trail and headed back up it—toward the villa far above him. There was a good chance Rojas was in his vehicle with his soldiers, coming down the road toward him. Jake had a plan. Maybe it would work. Leaping over a number of fallen logs, he headed toward the main dirt road, less than a tenth of a mile away.

As he did, he heard a sound that made his skin

crawl. The thump, thump, thump of shells being shot from the 30 mm cannon on the Kamov ripped through the jungle—right at him. Blasts of white-hot light exploded around him. Jake threw up his hands and dived for cover. Trees shattered. Splinters shrieked through the air like hundreds of needles being blasted at him. Dirt and rock vomited upward like gray-and-black geysers all around him. Burying his head beneath his arms, Jake felt rocks and dirt savagely pelt him. He groaned as something hard and heavy struck him in the lower back.

Struggling to get up, he heard more thudding thumps of cannon shells being fired at him. Sprinting to the left, across land torn up with small craters and leaning trees, Jake again headed for the main road. Breath torn from him, gun in hand, he ran as hard as he could. More cannon shells struck, but not near him. They were being aimed somewhere else....

And then something happened. He heard the Kamov turning away from him. Sliding to a halt, Jake spun around. His eyes widened. The Kamov was moving back down the hill—right toward the ravine. Why? Had the pilot gotten its IR on Tal and Ana? Sobbing for breath, Jake ran as hard as he could down the hill after the retreating helicopter.

He'd gone only two hundred feet when he saw why the Kamov had stopped hunting him. Ana was standing in a small clearing, in full view, her pistol aimed upward, firing away at the Kamov!

"No! Damn...no," he sobbed as he ran. Ana was standing there, legs spread apart for balance, her face impassive, her pistol raised defiantly to the sky. She was challenging the Kamov directly. She'd die.

Jake screamed her name. "*Ana!* Get out of there! Get out!" But his voice was drowned out by the Kamov, which was now slowing to a hover. The pilot had Ana in his sites now. Running and stumbling through the thick underbrush and around trees, Jake knew he'd never make it in time to where Ana stood. He passed a small opening in the canopy. *Wait!* Sliding to a halt, he leaped backward.

The fuselage of the black Kamov was accessible! He couldn't even wait to steady his pistol against something solid. Aiming for the side window, Jake fired off four quick shots. This time the bullets didn't deflect. This time, they shattered the Plexiglas on the right side of the cockpit. Jake gave a yell of triumph. Had he hit the pilot? He stood there panting, holding the gun in his hand.

The Kamov suddenly moved—toward him again. *Damn!* Jake caught Ana's gaze. He yelled at her.

"Get out of here! Get to the ravine!" He gestured wildly, pointing toward the ravine.

Ana heard Jake's deep, emphatic voice. The Kamov's engines drowned out whatever he was screaming, but she saw the terror in his eyes and knew he wanted her out of there. Hesitating, Ana saw the Kamov turn toward Jake. They had to buy time!

Just then, Ana heard another voice. A woman's voice. It was Tal, calling up to her from the ravine. Ana couldn't look. Her gaze was narrowed on the stalking gunship, which was now siting on Jake. Why wouldn't Jake move? He had to run! Ana didn't want him to die. Gulping hard, she shrieked at Jake to run, but he didn't hear her.

Ana lifted her pistol and fired the last four bullets into the left side panel of the Kamov cockpit. The window shattered outward in a spray of rainbow colors at it caught the sunlight and fell earthward. Had she wounded the pilot?

No! A scream lurched from Ana. She saw the Kamov firing cannon shells in Jake's direction. He dived for cover.

With shaking hands, Ana quickly released the spent cartridges and slammed another clip into the butt of her pistol. She stood and started firing again at the Kamov, to try and draw him off Jake. It worked!

Ana released the emptied clip and slammed her third and final one into the pistol. She saw the Kamov turn—toward her. Leaping out of the clearing, Ana headed down toward the ravine at top speed.

It was then that Ana saw Tal standing in the middle of the ravine, in plain view. She'd told her to hide, not be a target! Speeding up, Ana raced wildly down the hill, screaming at Tal to take cover. The Kamov suddenly moved forward. The pilot had spotted Tal out in the open!

Ana no longer thought, she only reacted. She knew what had to be done. Racing down into the dry ravine, filled with dust kicked up in thick, yellow clouds by the Kamov's approach, she headed directly for Tal. The woman was stricken, frozen with fear. Lunging toward Tal, Ana pushed her heavily to the ground, to the embankment.

It was then she heard a sound that made her cry

out. The Kamov had loosed a rocket directly at them! Ana had thrown her body over Tal's to protect her as they hit and rolled to the hard, unforgiving ground. In the next instant, they were both lifted violently into the air. The explosive concussion ripped into Ana's ears. She screamed. Tal cried out. And then darkness deluged Ana and she heard nothing more.

Jake slowly got to his feet. He saw the Kamov firing a rocket into the ravine. Dazed and semiconscious, he gasped for breath, heedless of the blood running out of his nose and mouth. Cannon shells had exploded all around him. Crying out Ana's and Tal's names, Jake staggered forward. He tripped. He fell. And then he heard the Kamov once more turning—toward him.

He was out of ammunition. He was helpless. Jake was ready to die. Below, he could see a huge cloud of yellow dust rising into the air where the rocket had been fired into the ravine. Where Tal and Ana had taken cover... Tears flooded into his eyes. Anger surged through him.

To his amazement, as he leaped down toward the ravine, the Kamov suddenly revved its engines and headed away again. Shaking his head in puzzlement, Jake staggered toward the area where Tal and Ana had been waiting for rescue.

And then he saw why. Two black Apache helicopters were blazing down from higher altitudes, aimed right at the fleeing Kamov. Then he saw the Cobra coming—their rescue ship.

Stumbling, Jake holstered the pistol and concentrated on running. Rounding a bend, he saw the dust beginning to clear. Where the rocket had landed a huge crater had been created. And up on the embankment were his sister and Ana. A cry lurched from his parched throat. Ana was leaning over Tal, who was lying on her back. Tal was screaming in pain.

As Jake raced up, his eyes widened with horror. His sister's right thigh had been torn open, the stark white bone of her broken femur sticking out of the bleeding flesh. Dropping to his knees, he saw that Ana was doing what she could for Tal. His sister was in shock, her eyes black and glassy looking.

"Take it easy...easy...." Jake rasped. He put one shaking hand on Tal's shoulder as she flailed wildly and tried to sit up.

Ana jerked a look at him. Jake's face was bloodied and cut. She quickly took her belt from around her waist and slid it under Tal's thigh above the compound fracture. In the background, she could hear the Cobra's beating blades as it came in for a landing.

"Jake, get to the Cobra!" Ana cried, the noise of the landing helicopter almost drowning her out. "We need a stretcher! They've got one on board. Hurry!"

He hesitated, then got to his feet. The Cobra had just landed a hundred feet away, viciously kicking up dust as it powered down. He saw one pilot up front. A short, copper-skinned woman who looked Peruvian leaped out of the opening door on the side of the helicopter. She was dressed in a black, body-fitting uniform with no patches or identification. Her black hair was twisted in a knot at the base of her neck. The expression on her face was grim. Jake ran toward her as she ducked beneath the whirling rotor blades.

"I need a stretcher!" Jake yelled at the woman.

"How many down?" she yelled back.

"One. My sister. Leg fracture."

The woman nodded and hurried back to the Cobra. Jake went with her. In moments, he and the woman had the portable stretcher and a paramedic bag in their hands. They ran back to where Ana was leaning over Tal and trying to console her.

Ana looked up. "Angel!"

Angel Paredes grinned tightly and nodded to Ana. She dropped the stretcher and knelt down to examine the injured woman. "Hi there, Lieutenant. Looks like you've seen some trouble."

Ana wiped her bloody nose. Her ears had blood leaking out of them as well because of the rocket concussion. "Yeah, a little hell on earth. Can we help you?"

Paredes, a sergeant and paramedic, quickly looked up after examining Tal's injured leg. "Yeah. Get my traction splint out of the back of the Cobra, will you, Lieutenant? We've got to get this bone back in her leg before we start transport or it's a no go." Angel flew into her paramedic pack and located a shot of morphine, which she gave Tal. It would lessen her pain almost immediately.

Jake watched tensely as he sat at his sister's head, his hands on her shoulders to stabilize her. Tal was moaning now. Her eyes were half-closed and glazed looking. She was weakly flailing her arms. Blood was pumping thickly around the stark white end of her shattered femur.

Jake wanted to cry. He wanted to scream out in

rage at what the Kamov had done. Would Tal die? He anxiously watched Angel throw a blood pressure cuff around her arm and take a reading. Judging from the Peruvian woman's expression, it wasn't a good one.

Ana came back, panting as she held the traction splint out to Angel. "Tell me what to do, Angel."

Quickly, Angel told them how to help her. In no time, she had the traction device on Tal's injured leg. At the count of three, Angel expertly and quickly pulled the femur out of its position and settled it back into Tal's leg. Tal wasn't feeling any pain now, thanks to the shot of morphine. She was barely conscious as Angel wrapped the leg, and the three of them, on her count, transferred Tal to the stretcher.

Jake took one end of the stretcher. He saw Ana flinch as she leaned down to take the other end. Her face went ashen. It was then that he realized she, too, was hurt. How bad? He couldn't tell. Time was of the essence. Tal was unconscious now.

Paredes handed Ana her bag. "You carry this," she said quickly. Looking at Jake, she reached for the other end of the stretcher. "Let's saddle up!"

Once inside the tight confines of the Cobra, Jake stayed out of the way as best he could. Paredes slid the door shut and patted the woman helicopter pilot on the shoulder. The sergeant quickly put on her helmet, which was hooked up to the intercabin radio system, and told the pilot to head straight for Cusco. Also to radio ahead and tell the hospital staff they had an incoming emergency flight patient on board and to be ready to receive them on the landing pad. The pilot hitched her thumb upward. Ana climbed between them and sat in the left seat of the Cobra. She donned a helmet, too, and strapped in.

Jake felt the Cobra break contact with the earth. His gaze was riveted on Tal. Angel had covered her with several blankets to keep the shock at bay. She worked frantically over the leg to control the bleeding. She enlisted Jake's help by having him press the heel of his hand where Tal's leg connected to her body. It was there that the femoral artery lay, and by putting a lot of pressure on it, they could slow blood supply to that leg and stop some of the continuing blood loss.

The Cobra shook and shuddered as it gained altitude. Jake's world centered on his pale, shocked-looking sister. Once he looked up between the metal panels to see Ana talking and pointing out the windshield, but because he didn't have a helmet on, he didn't know what was being said. Was the Kamov coming after them? He felt his heart pound with another surge of adrenaline at that thought.

How was Ana? She was white-faced, her gold skin leached out. He tried to see if there was blood anywhere else other than her face, but he could see nothing. Yet her full lips were compressed into a tight line. What if Ana had internal injuries? They'd taken a direct rocket attack. Worried for her, Jake felt helpless. He watched as Angel worked with fierce energy and care over his sister. She finally got the bleeding stopped, and told him to release the pressure on Tal's upper leg.

Taking his hand away, Jake rubbed his face. He

was muddy, and a little blood was still leaking out of his nose. Giving the paramedic an inquiring look, he leaned over Tal and yelled, "Is she going to be okay?"

Paredes nodded. She patted him on the shoulder. "What about you? Are you okay?" she yelled back over the din of the chopper blades.

Jake nodded. They had to scream in order to hear one another above the noise created by the shaking, shuddering Cobra. For anyone without a protective helmet on, talking was almost impossible.

"Check out Ana," he yelled.

"What?" Paredes put her hand to the side of her helmet.

Jake roared, "Ana! She's hurt!"

Paredes nodded. She tapped her wrist where her watch was. "Twenty minutes to Cusco. Hang on. I'll take a check on her after we land."

Ana remained in the Cobra as the medical team from the Cusco hospital placed Tal on a gurney and hurried her in through the back doors to an emergency room. Jake had reached out for her, to ask if she was all right, and Ana had nodded and given him a game smile. Ana had seen the terror and worry in his eyes for his sister, and she'd told him to go with Tal, that she'd be along shortly.

Cam, the pilot, shut off the engine and gave her a cursory look. "Ana? You okay? You look like hell warmed over."

With a grimace, Ana nodded. "I think I busted some ribs. I'll be okay...."

"You'd better get in there, then," Cam said, shutting down all the other systems. "I'll go with you."

Ana nodded, knowing there was no reason to wait on the landing pad. The two Apache helicopters would never come to Cusco. Captain Stevenson, who was flying one, had ordered them back to Black Jaguar base, deep in the jungles of Peru.

Cam pulled the helmet off her head, her thick red hair tumbling around her shoulders. Her forest-green eyes were worried looking as she eased out of the tight cockpit and into the cabin. She waited for Ana to unstrap herself and disembark.

Ana found her hands shaking badly. She could barely release the harness. Setting the helmet aside, she slowly got up. Fire arced up through the right side of her rib cage. As she sucked in a breath, the pain increased. All Ana could do was take shallow breaths or risk that awful knifelike pain ripping up her side. Wrapping her hand around her right ribs, she made her way out of the Cobra and onto the concrete slab. They were three hundred feet from the red brick hospital's entrance.

"Okay?" Cam asked gently as she put her arm around Ana's waist to steady her.

Ana sighed. "I'll be okay. Just keep an arm on me, Cam. My knees are starting to feel a little wobbly right now."

Cam grinned and walked her slowly toward the entrance on the concrete sidewalk that lead from the landing circle. "Hey, if I'd had a Kamov firing a rocket at me, I wouldn't be feeling very chipper right now, either."

It hurt to laugh. With a grimace, Ana began to feel the tiredness of the world settle on her shoulders. Every step was a struggle. The adrenaline was leaving her now, and she felt weakness attacking her. The pain in her side increased proportionately when she crept forward with mincing steps, trying to minimize it as much as possible.

As Jake headed down to emergency, he was torn. He wanted to leave Tal's side and go find Ana, but he didn't dare. Once Tal was taken into surgery, however, he started to hunt Ana down. He noticed that the hospital was small, clean and efficient. The nursing staff and doctors looked at him in shock as he headed down the sparkling white hall toward the main desk. Jake knew he looked a sight. The mud had dried on his clothes, his face and fingers. And dried blood was caked across his chest.

As he came to the nurses' station, he saw the red-haired pilot dressed in her black flight suit coming out of a room down the hall. Jake bypassed the desk and headed straight for her. He saw the nurses whispering in lowered voices and pointing at the woman pilot as she stood in the corridor, her helmet dangling from her left hand, her bright, burnished hair loose across her shoulders. She gave him a brisk nod of greeting as he approached.

"Hi, we've not been introduced yet. I'm Cam. You're Jake Travers, right?"

Jake took her hand, finding her grip surprisingly firm. She looked to be in her mid-twenties, with an oval face, serious-looking dark green eyes and a slight, friendly smile on her wide mouth. "Yeah, I am. Is Ana in there? I've been trying to find out about her, how she is...."

Cam nodded. "Yeah, she's in there getting her ribs taped up."

Jake frowned. "Broken ribs?"

"Yeah. She's gonna be fine, though, so don't worry."

"Can I see her?"

Cam's smile increased. "I'm sure she'd like to see you, Mr. Travers."

Opening the door, Jake quietly walked in. The nurse was just finishing up the taping and had helped Ana into a light blue gown. She was sitting on the side of a bed, her legs dangling. She looked up. Her face glowed as she saw him.

"Jake!"

Just hearing Ana's soft voice sent a ribbon of heat through him. Jake managed a lopsided smile and lifted his hand. "I've been trying to find you. How are you?"

Ana thanked the nurse and slowly got into bed, pulling the covers up with her left arm. Right now, with her cracked ribs, it hurt to stretch out her right arm. "I'm doing better." Ana saw that he was still muddy and bloodied from their standoff with the Kamov. "I'll bet people are looking at you funny." She managed a one-cornered smile.

"I probably look like death walking the halls." Jake halted near her bed. He waited until the nurse was gone. Ana was clean. She'd taken a shower, her dark hair thick and damp around her shoulders. There were dark smudges beneath her eyes and he could tell she was in pain by the way her lips were compressed.

There was so much he wanted to say to her, and time didn't seem to be on their side. Opening his muddy hand, Jake said, "Broken ribs?"

"Yes. When the Kamov fired the rocket, it blasted us into the air. I lost consciousness as we were going up. When I woke up, I was lying across a small tree trunk." She tenderly touched her ribs. "That's when I think I fractured them." Her brows fell. "Enough of me. What about your sister? How's Tal doing?" Ana saw the grimness in Jake's eyes and the deep crease marks bracketing his mouth. She reached out and slid her fingers into his, not caring if he was clean or dirty. She needed to feel him, to have him near.

"They have her in surgery right now." Giving her fingers a slight squeeze, he released her. "I'm dirty, Ana." What he'd like to do was kiss the hell out of her. Right now, Jake needed her like he'd never needed another woman before. He saw the tender look in her eyes, and saw that she wanted to kiss him, too. Rubbing his face, his beard stiff beneath his fingertips, he muttered, "Let me find a hotel near here. I need to get cleaned up. I've put a call in to Morgan Trayhern at Perseus for help. The surgeon said that Tal is going to need a specialist. I don't want her recovering here in Peru. I want to take her home, to the States."

Ana's heart fell. Pain ravaged her chest and she avoided his dark, exhausted gaze. "Y-yes…Tal should go home…and you with her. She's going to need you, Jake. What she just went through…well, I know how close you two are and she's going to need someone to talk to, a shoulder to cry on...."

Jake nodded wearily. "Listen, so much has happened.... I just don't have the time right now to talk more, Ana." He searched her grave face. "Do you understand?"

Ana understood clearly. Nodding, she compressed her lips and whispered, "Jake, go see your sister. Be with her. Right now, Tal needs you." Reaching out, Ana settled her hand on his arm and squeezed it gently. Her heart ached. Whatever was between them would be left unspoken. It wasn't the right time or place for such a discussion. "I'll be okay."

Standing there for a moment, Jake realized that whatever problems he'd had with Ana's warrior side were laid to rest. She'd proved herself to him in the fire of combat. Still in a state of shock over her bravery and cool thinking during the Kamov attack, he realized that all facets of Ana made her who she was. He needed her. All of her, without any more questioning. She was a woman. She could be his wife. Mother to his children. A fierce, confident warrior who would fight at his side through all of life's ups and downs. His trust of Ana was solid. She had proved to him that women belonged in combat just as men did. Without her help out there earlier, Tal would be dead—and so would he. Aching to speak to her, Jake moved away from her bed. Time wasn't on their side. At least, not yet.

Chapter Nine

Ana tried to console herself as she lay somewhere between sleep and wakefulness. If she tried to breathe deeply, her right side felt like it was on fire. Luckily, the ribs she'd cracked were at the base of her rib cage and therefore could be wrapped. The tight adhesive bandage helped a great deal, but breathing deeply wasn't in the cards.

The private room she was in was quiet. Pale blue curtains hung over a window that had venetian blinds drawn across it, and slats of early afternoon sunlight filtered in, making her feel a bit better. There was a television on the wall but she didn't feel like watching it. No, her heart, her mind, were centered on Jake— and how she felt about him. He'd hesitantly left her side hours ago.

How could she have fallen in love with him? Ana lay there picking nervously at the light blue coverlet, her brows knitted. She barely knew Jake, and yet he'd risked his life for her and his sister. He was a man of valor and of honor. Compressing her lips, Ana felt restless. The last place she wanted to be was in bed. And how was Tal? Was she out of surgery yet, after that awful leg fracture she'd suffered? Ana imagined Jake walking the halls outside the surgery lounge, worried sick about his sister.

"Enough of this," Ana muttered, dragging off the covers. Her muddy clothes had been washed, dried, and now hung in the closet. Moving gingerly, her hand pressed protectively against her fractured ribs, Ana opened the door. She couldn't stand being in bed. She had to find out about Tal…and she wanted to be with Jake. Reaching for the hanger that held her clothes, Ana grimaced. Maya wouldn't let her fly with broken ribs. She would be grounded for six weeks. That didn't make her feel any better, because her sister pilots would have to fill in for her. That would put even more pressure and demand on them than they already had. And Ana knew from the years she'd spent at the base helping Maya that the work was demanding and tiring.

As she dragged her clothes off the hanger, one article at a time, Ana grimaced. Her friends would have to carry her part of the flight load, and that made her feel worse. They were all flying too much and not getting enough rest. Sleep deprivation was an evil that hung over the base and was a constant threat to their alertness. Out there in the skies over the jungle, the

Kamovs just waited to jump them. And a pilot tired because of too much time on duty could make deadly mistakes. Exhaustion could make the pilot vulnerable to attack—and in danger of dying.

Unhappily, Ana struggled out of the light blue gown and into her clothes. Leaning over to try and lace up her muddy hiking boots was the hardest part. Looking in the mirror in the bathroom, she saw that her hair was now dry. Managing to awkwardly lift the brush with her left hand she brushed her dark black hair until it shone with reddish highlights and lay like a soft, luxuriant cloak around her shoulders.

Turning, she felt her heart lift momentarily. Just the thought of being with Jake once again made Ana feel better. She couldn't jerk the heavy door open. Instead, she used her left hand to get it ajar, then wedged her boot between it and the jamb. Eventually she got it open enough to slip out to the highly polished, white-tiled hall. The odor of antiseptic filled the air, and Ana wrinkled her nose, hating the smell. She didn't like hospitals, either. She walked slowly and carefully down the hall, holding her side with her hand.

Jake was pouring himself a fifth cup of coffee from the urn in the surgery lounge when he heard someone enter. Thinking it was the surgeon finally come to see him, he turned, then froze momentarily. Ana stood at the entrance, her brow wrinkled, her eyes dark with pain. He set the cup down.

"Why aren't you in bed?" he demanded.

Ana smiled slightly. Jake had showered, shaved and was now in a set of newly purchased clothes: a pair of jeans and a gray-and-brown alpaca sweater, which outlined his magnificent shoulders and chest. Ana's heart thudded in her breast. Her *chalina* was now clean and dry, and he was wearing it around his neck. She wanted to cry. She wanted to hope that it meant something, a symbol. But did it really? Jake was *norteamericano* and even though he knew the *chalina* custom, that didn't mean he was committed as a man from South America might be if he wore it. "I'm not a bed kind of person. How's Tal? Have you heard anything yet?" Ana moved into the room, toward where Jake was standing. She saw the worry in his eyes and knew it was for his sister.

"No," he grumped. How beautiful Ana looked. Aside from the tension around her mouth and her hand pressed against her injured side, no one would be able to tell what she'd gone through just hours before. Yet Jake knew she must still be in shock over all of it, just as he was. "It's been three hours. What the hell are they doing in there?"

Ana gave him a tender look. Jake's hands were shaking badly as he put sugar into the cup of coffee. His mouth was a tight slash and his broad brow was deeply furrowed, out of concern for Tal, she knew. Reaching out with her left hand, Ana felt driven to touch Jake's upper arm. She needed to touch Jake. The alpaca sweater was soft beneath her fingertips.

"She's going to be okay. I feel it in my heart, Jake. It was a bad break. The doctors probably had a lot of bone splinters and fragments to search for. At least, that's what Angel mentioned just before we landed. And there was a lot of dirt in her wound. They probably have to flush it again and again to make sure there isn't one iota of debris left, or it will cause massive infection. They're going to take their time.'' She patted him gently.

Almost miraculously, Ana saw Jake's mouth soften at the corners and his brow smooth out a bit. It had never occurred to her until now just how much she could affect him. It made her feel good. Ana forced herself to stop touching him.

''I could use some coffee, too, please?''

Jake gave her a sidelong glance. ''Sure. Milk? Sugar?''

''Both.''

''We're still running on raw adrenaline,'' he muttered as he poured coffee into the paper cup.

Ana leaned against the wall near the table and voraciously absorbed the sight of Jake into her heart. How could she have fallen in love with him? When did it happen? Could love happen so quickly? She was unsure, and felt as if she was floundering. One thing she was certain about was that Jake would leave her as soon as Tal was able to be transported by air back to North America. Tears flooded Ana's eyes, surprising her. Looking away, she grappled with her unexpected reaction. Swallowing convulsively, she finally managed to contain her emotions, and turned back to him. He was handing her the cup of coffee, a strange look in his eyes.

''Thanks,'' she murmured, taking it.

''How are *you* feeling? You look pale,'' Jake noted as he walked with her to the red plastic couch and sat down near her. Ana sat carefully and very straight.

"I'm okay," she said. Giving him a wry look, she added, "And you? How are *you* doing?"

Sipping the hot coffee, his elbows resting on his massive thighs, Jake said, "Physically I've got a lot of bruises, but nothing's broken." Giving her a sour smile, he added, "I don't know why. That Kamov was thunking out 30 mm cannon shells at me like candy. I thought for sure I was going to die. It was just a matter of when."

Ana set the coffee down on the table beside the couch. She couldn't help herself, she needed Jake's nearness. Reaching out, she touched his arm again. To her surprise he put his cup down, enclosed her hand in his own and sat back. Tipping his head back, Jake sprawled out, his long legs in front of him beneath the coffee table, her hand held firmly in his.

"*This* is what I needed," he murmured, closing his eyes. "You."

Ana leaned back, their shoulders touching, their hands wrapped together. "I was missing you, too," she admitted in a low tone. Her heart ached with grief. Jake was going to leave her. Did she have the courage to tell him what lay in her heart? Would it make a difference? No, because Jake would go home to take care of Tal. And Tal was going to need him more than she. Tal would still be shell-shocked by the violence and trauma she'd experienced at Rojas's hands.

Ana would not ask Jake to stay. Under the circumstances, he must take care of his family first. She would make the same decision herself. Compressing her lips, Ana decided not to speak of what was in her heart. Family came first. His responsibility to Tal, his support of her healing was most important.

Jake's mouth twitched and he rolled his head in Ana's direction, barely opening his eyes. Ana's hand was small and slender in comparison to his. It was damp and cool. Squeezing it gently, he whispered, "I don't know what I was afraid of more, Ana—losing you or Tal. I didn't want either of you hurt…but when it was happening, when that Kamov was stalking us…well, a lot of things ran through my head and heart."

Ana hung on every huskily spoken word. She saw the warmth in Jake's eyes and greedily absorbed it. "Your first duty is to Tal," she said in a choked voice. "Tal was beaten up…maybe worse, I don't know. She's going to need you, Jake, in many ways. The physical scars will heal pretty quickly. I'm more worried about her emotional scars. She's going to need someone strong and caring like you to help her cope with all of this. Someone she can trust."

Nodding, he said, "I've already talked to Morgan Trayhern. They're sending an air ambulance down here." He looked at his watch. "They'll be landing in Cusco in three hours. There's an emergency-trained physician on board. As soon as the docs here at the hospital say Tal can leave, we're flying her back to the States. I want to take her home, to my parents' farm in Iowa. I've been in touch with Mom and Dad. They know everything. They want Tal home to heal up. I agree with them."

"Good," Ana whispered, meaning it. "I've seen too many young women like Tal terrorized by drug lords. It's awful to be trapped, to be a plaything to them, at the whim of their violence and selfishness.''

''I...'' Jake scowled. He opened his eyes and sat up. ''I'm afraid Tal was raped. The look in her eyes...like a wild animal... I've never seen that look before, Ana. I'm afraid she's going to tell me that when she comes out of surgery.'' Wiping his mouth with the back of his hand, Jake rasped, ''I don't know how to help her on that. I'm a man....''

Sitting up, Ana turned toward him, her knee pressing against his thigh. She gripped his hand firmly. ''Listen to me, Jake, you're her *brother*. Yes, you're a man. And if Rojas or those other goons raped Tal, she might have a hard time at first because you *are* a man. But you've got a lot going for you,'' she whispered fervently. ''You're close to her. You shared so many good times together. Tal *loves* you, Jake. And she *trusts* you. That's the key in helping her. Just let her talk, okay? And get her help by locating a counselor or psychotherapist who has an office near your parents' farm. That and time will help her recover.''

Gazing up at her, Jake saw the anguish in Ana's wide, cinnamon eyes. ''Do you know how beautiful you are? From the heart outward?'' He was stunned by how deep his feelings for Ana ran, but he knew that, under the circumstances, he couldn't spill his heart out to her. Tal needed him, and would for a while. She might have a physical injury to heal from, but if she'd been raped, there was an even deeper, darker wound that would have to be addressed. Tal would need to heal in her spirit as well as her body in any case, due to all the violence and trauma she'd suffered.

"You're a very brave man," Ana said, her voice wobbling as she clung to his hand. "I couldn't stand the fact that you put yourself in danger for us. When I saw the Kamov hunting you, I couldn't let you face it alone...." She lowered her lashes, tears welling into her eyes. Above all, Jake couldn't see her cry. He mustn't.

Though he ached to take Ana into his arms, Jake squelched the desire. She looked raw and was obviously hurting. All he could do presently was hold her hand. "Brave? You were courageous. My heart dropped through my feet when I saw you standing out there in that clearing, trying to draw the Kamov off me." He shook his head. *To hell with it.* He lifted his hand and eased his fingers through her thick, luxuriant hair, then cupped her cheek. Guiding her chin upward, he saw that her eyes were dark and marred with pain. Her lower lip trembled.

"Listen...this isn't the time or place, Ana. So much has happened so fast, my head's still spinning. I want...I want to say so much to you...about the discoveries I've made, how I feel about you. But dammit, I can't! It's Tal.... I have to be there for her. I know you understand that." Reluctantly, he dropped his hand from her cheek. Yet he saw hope burning deeply in her eyes as his gaze locked with hers. When she lifted the corners of her suffering mouth in a slight smile, his heart wrenched.

"I know that," Ana said in a choked voice. "And

I accept that. Family is first. Always. That is the way of *campesinos*.''

''I don't want to leave here, leave you....'' He managed a twisted smile. ''Peru has grown on me more than I ever thought possible.''

''Well...'' Ana whispered, unable to hold his intense, burning gaze, ''maybe she'll call you back here someday....''

Jake stood the instant the surgeon, Dr. Ramone Salinas, entered the surgery lounge. The doctor took off his blue sterile cap from his balding head and went straight to them. Ana stood, her arm around Jake's waist to support him, no matter what the news was.

''Doctor?'' Jake's voice was low with tension. ''How's Tal?''

Salinas, a man in his fifties, with a silver goatee and narrow face, nodded deferentially. ''I'm sorry it took so long, Señor Travers, but your sister's compound fracture was very complicated. She is out of surgery now, and in recovery.'' Waving his thin, long hand, he said, ''There were many, many fine bone splinters and fragments that we had to search for. Several of her veins and an artery had to be spliced and repaired. She has lost some of the femur, the thigh bone, as you know it, and that leg will be roughly half an inch to an inch shorter than her other leg. She can, of course, compensate for that by wearing a shoe with a thicker sole. I'm sure you will have her talk to a specialist in *Norteamérica* when you take her home. Right now, she's coming out of anesthesia and her vital signs are strong and good.'' He smiled a little. ''You can go see her now, if you wish.''

Jake felt relief sheet through him like heat on a freezing day. ''Thank you, Doctor,'' he said, pumping the surgeon's hand fervently. Tears welled up in Jake's eyes, but he didn't care. Ana was looking up at him, her face alight with joy—for him. For Tal. She was so unselfish. He placed his arm around her proud shoulders.

''We'd like to see her, Dr. Salinas. Any problem with Ana coming with me?''

He frowned. ''She is family?''

Ana knew the rules. Only close relatives could see someone in recovery. She started to speak, but Jake gripped her shoulder gently.

''Yes, she is, Doctor.''

Salinas smiled briefly. ''Of course. Please, go see her. Just go down to the end of the hall and turn right. The recovery nurse will take you to her.''

Ana walked with Jake out of the room. He wouldn't let her go, and it felt good to be wrapped in his arm and walking at his side. Jake was careful of her broken ribs and shortened his stride to match hers. Ana was grateful.

''This is such great news,'' she said. How strong and supportive Jake's body was against hers. Ana hungered to simply have time to lay at his side and explore him, love him and give herself to him in all ways.

''I'm walking on air,'' he told her, his voice still wobbling with emotion. Turning at the end of the hall, they found themselves at another desk. Behind the desk was a glass-enclosed room with several patients on gurneys who had recently come out of surgery. A number of nurses were going from one gurney to another checking each patient in turn. Jake stretched to his full height and saw Tal's ruffled blond hair on the last gurney in the line. He could barely make out his sister's pale face. When one of the nurses in dark green scrubs came out, Ana spoke to her in Spanish and told them who they were. The nurse smiled and gestured for them to follow her. Inside the cool, air-conditioned room, which smelled strongly of anesthesia and other hospital odors, Jake stood on one side of Tal's gurney, Ana on the other. He leaned down and gently curved his hand across her tousled blond hair.

"Tal? It's Jake. We're here. You're okay. Everything went fine, Sis. You're here in Cusco, Peru. In a hospital." Jake saw Tal's lashes flutter. His heart wrenched as she slowly turned her head toward him. The bruising beneath her right eye, the swelling of her nose and cheek, made his blood run hot with rage again. Tal had been beaten a number of times, there was no question. Gently stroking her hair, he leaned over the gurney and put his other hand on her thickly blanketed shoulder. As she opened her eyes to slits, he smiled down at her.

"Hi, Sleeping Beauty."

Tal's mouth opened. Her lower lip was badly chapped, but she managed to hike one corner. "Jake...you're here...."

"Yeah, I am." Jake looked up. "And so is Ana. You remember her?"

Tal frowned, her thin eyebrows knitting slowly. She closed her eyes and moved her lips together. "No..."

"She's groggy, Jake," Ana said quietly. Leaning over with a damp cloth, she gently patted it against Tal's dry lips. "She's probably thirsty, too."

Jake was grateful for Ana's presence. She seemed to know about these things. As he looked down, he saw that Tal's leg was heavily bandaged, and held in place by a series of pulleys suspended above the gurney. She had IVs in both arms. Just watching Ana administer to Tal broke his heart. He was going to be leaving here soon. Ana would be left behind. Jake didn't want that to happen.

Grimly, he shoved away his personal feelings, the ache in his heart, and settled all his attention on Tal.

Jake made sure that Tal had been transferred safely aboard Perseus's Learjet and had the physician onboard attending her before he exited the plane. He saw Ana waiting for him at the bottom of the stairs. The morning was cool, with clouds hanging over the valley where Cusco lay. The mountains were dark brown, bare of much vegetation at this twelve-thousand-foot elevation. Off to the right, he saw a civilian helicopter and Captain Maya Stevenson, dressed in civilian clothes, slowly walking toward them. Ana would be flown back to Agua Caliente, the tiny town at the foot of Machu Picchu. From there, another civilian helicopter would pick them up and fly them fifty miles into the jungle and back to their hidden base. Ana didn't want to stay in Cusco, and

Jake didn't blame her. All her friends were at the base.

When Jake looked down at Ana's upturned face, his heart cringed. Today, she wore jeans, hiking boots, a dark brown leather jacket and a soft pink alpaca sweater with a cowl neck that showed off her beautiful face and slender neck. Her dark hair lay in a thick coverlet about her shoulders. He saw the sorrow in her cinnamon eyes.

His gaze settled hotly on her lips. From time to time over the past week, they'd shared sweet, lingering kisses. And yet neither had talked about the future. The past seven days had been a bittersweet heaven and hell for him, and for Ana as well, he was sure. They'd spent a lot of time with Tal, who was still in shock but slowly recovering from her injuries. Her leg was the least of her problems, Jake was discovering. She had been raped by Rojas a number of times, so Jake knew now that he had his work cut out for him. Thanks to Ana and their long discussions, he had a better understanding of Tal and what kind of emotions to expect after her trauma. He felt more confident about being there for his sister and getting her qualified help once he got her home.

Reaching out, Jake murmured, "It's time, Ana...." He felt her fingers slide into his as he halted at the bottom of the stairs. Around them, large airliners that plied their trade between Lima and Cusco were trundling down the runway toward takeoff. It was only 6:00 a.m., and the chill that hung around the international airport was bone deep.

"I know...." Ana put on her best face.

Jake looked beyond her. "That's Captain Stevenson coming to pick you up?" Tall and proud, the commanding officer moved with a confidence he rarely saw in women. And to top it off, she was drop-dead gorgeous even at this distance, with her thick, black hair flowing across her shoulders. He reminded himself there were women warriors in the world. Ana had shown him that. She was a proud example as far as he was concerned.

"Yes." Ana tried to ignore the pain in her racing heart. "She'll take me home, Jake."

"Home," he mused as he placed his arms around her and brought her gently against him. Her hips settled against his. Burning heat flowed through his lower body. How badly Jake wanted to love Ana. As she tipped her head upward, he saw tears matted in her thick black lashes. "You've been my home away from home, Ana...." And she had. In the past week, Jake had found out just how emotionally strong and nurturing Ana could be. When he'd found out Tal had been raped, he'd fled the room. He'd gone off to an isolated stairwell on Tal's floor, and sat down and cried. Ana had found him. He'd been angry and frustrated and hurt by Tal's admittance. Ana had quietly come and sat down next to him, put her slender arm around his shoulders and held him gently while he cried for his sister and her pain.

Ana hadn't said anything. She'd just let him cry and get out the venom and hatred he felt for Tal's attackers. Jake wanted to kill every one of them. He hurt for Tal. Even though he couldn't imagine what had happened to her, he could see the devastation it had wrought on her. His once sunny, ebullient sister was now fearful, withdrawn and jumpy. She didn't sleep well at night. She had nightmares. He'd sobbed out his hatred about it to Ana. And all she'd done was hold him and rock him with her womanly strength and tenderness. It was then that Jake knew he loved her with a fervency that burned in his soul.

He looked deeply into Ana's eyes now and saw the tears glimmering in them. Captain Stevenson halted a good ten feet away and waited patiently, an understanding look on her clean, proud features. Jake caressed Ana's shoulders tenderly. "You're my *real* home, Ana. You know that, don't you?" How much he wanted to say. And how little time was left to say it. Jake knew their lives were never going to cross. It was just as well he'd resigned his commission in the army because Tal needed him, and he wouldn't go rushing back to his post under the circumstances. No, he'd be staying at the farm to be with her, to help her heal, if he could. He could promise Ana nothing. Nothing.

Her heart broke. Ana leaned her head against Jake's broad shoulder. Hot tears dripped down her cheeks. She felt his hands moving gently across her shoulders and down to caress her spine, carefully because of her rib injury. Today he wore her *chalina*. What did it all mean? Confused, Ana whispered, "The heart has many homes, Jake."

He laughed roughly and pressed a kiss to her hair. "Mine has only one, Ana. You." Sliding his hand beneath her chin, he made her look up at him. His heart contracted with anguish as he saw the paths of tears down her wan cheeks. Her eyes were filled with anguish. "I've got to go...."

"I know...."

"You mean so much to me, Ana...."

More tears fell. His face blurred before her. "I—I know. I feel the same, Jake...but Tal needs you more than ever now. You can help her heal...."

He smiled down at Ana as he slid his hand across her jaw and angled her head toward his descending one. "You've helped to heal me, you know...." He settled his mouth gently upon hers and felt her quiver. Her left arm slid across his shoulder and she pressed herself against him. She tasted sweet and warm. How brave she was. Jake felt her returning fire, felt her heart being given to him. Ana was as honest as she was pragmatic. She knew he had to leave.

Easing away from her lips, the taste of her salty tears upon his mouth, he framed her face with his hands. "I'm keeping the *chalina,* Ana. As a reminder of what we shared." His fingers tightened briefly around her face. "Do you hear me?"

She barely nodded her head, unable to stop crying. "Y-yes, I hear you, Jake." A huge sob welled up through her chest and jammed in her throat. His hands were gentle upon her and she ached to speak of her love for him.

Jake grimaced and looked away for a moment, his eyes alive with anguish.

One of the pilots came to the entrance and called Jake by name.

He had to leave. Ana released him. She patted the soft, rainbow-colored scarf that hung down his chest.

Wiping her eyes, she whispered, "Take care of yourself?"

Caressing her damp cheek, he turned and placed his foot on the step leading into the Learjet. "Yes, sweetheart, I will...."

Ana backed away. She watched Jake wave to her one last time and then disappear into the jet. The whirring sounds of the stairs being pulled up and the door locking into place against the Learjet fuselage made her heart cringe. Soon the engines would start up. Ana turned and walked toward Maya, who had a sad look on her features. More tears squeezed out of Ana's eyes. She didn't try to stop them now. The whine of the Lear's engines began. Jake was leaving. He would be gone—forever. Ana had no fantasy about him returning. Not ever.

As Ana came over to Maya, she saw her C.O. reach out with her hand to grip her shoulder.

"I'm sorry, Ana."

Nodding, afraid to speak because she'd sob, Ana kept on walking toward the helicopter in the distance. She heard the Lear's engines heighten. Ana didn't—couldn't—look back. She couldn't stand to see Jake's face at the window. Her heart thrashed with pain. As she reached the Bell helicopter, opened the copilot's door on the left side and slid in, she sobbed unabashedly, her face buried in her hands. She leaned over, the pain so great that she wanted to double up, but couldn't. She vaguely heard the other door open and then close, and felt Maya's quiet presence in the right seat, the pilot's seat.

Trying to get a hold on herself, Ana felt Maya pressing several tissues into her hand.

"Life is hell," Maya muttered. She waved to the man who removed the chalks from around the wheels of the Bell helicopter. Busying herself with starting up the engines, she glanced sadly at Ana once more.

Straightening, Ana mopped her eyes and blew her nose. She saw the Learjet trundling slowly down the runway to the takeoff point. Her heart felt squeezed by a huge, invisible hand. "Yes," she whispered brokenly, "it's hell on earth..." And she started sobbing again.

"Get your harness on," Maya told her gently. "It's time to go home, Ana."

Home. Jake had said *she* was his home. What did that mean? Ana was aching too much, caught in the storm of her love and loss of Jake, to figure it out. As the Bell's rotors began to turn, the engines revving with a whine, Ana strapped herself in. Just as the Learjet took off and headed north, the helicopter took off and headed westward, toward Agua Caliente.

Ana sat there, the tissues gripped in her clenched hands, her eyes blurring continually with tears. The dark brown of the mountains quickly slipped past as the helicopter descended in altitude from twelve thousand to six thousand feet toward Agua Caliente, an hour away from Cusco.

Finally, Ana put on the headset. She saw Maya give her worried glances from time to time. Even though she wore dark green aviator glasses, Ana could feel her C.O.'s caring.

"You fell in love with him, didn't you?" Maya asked.

Nodding, Ana whispered, "Yes. But I don't know how, Maya." Ana pressed her hand to her aching heart. "I don't know how...there wasn't enough time... It's *loco*—crazy...."

Maya chuckled, her full mouth parting in a derisive smile. "Well, I'm not one to know about *real* love. That's never happened to me. I thought I was in love once, but that got shattered in a hurry. So I'm not the one to tell you one way or another about how much time it takes to fall in love."

Sniffling, Ana blew her nose and wiped her eyes of the last of the tears. She knew she'd cry many more times over Jake leaving her.

Above them, the sky was a pale blue color. The dark brown ridges, and the *apus*—the snow-capped mountains in the distance—gave her some feeling of comfort because she'd been raised in Rainbow Valley, over which they now flew.

"I gave him my *chalina*."

"I saw. Does he know what that means?"

"Yes."

Maya shifted uncomfortably in her seat. "I don't know, Ana. *Norteamericano* men don't come highly recommended in my book. They don't know our customs, our belief system down here."

Ana bowed her head. She knew Maya was trying to tell her not to expect Jake to honor the *chalina*, or what it meant. She was right, of course. Jake might like her, might try to honor her people's traditions, but Maya's grimly spoken words had a lot of experience behind them. Maya, who was Brazilian, had been adopted as a child by a North American couple and knew of what she spoke.

"I know…" Ana managed to reply finally. Wiping her eyes a final time, she swiveled her head automatically to look for Kamovs. They were in a civilian helicopter, so they were safe, but that didn't stop her from giving in to her training and strong survival skills.

"All my run-ins with *norteamericano* men have been a disaster," Maya growled. She moved the Bell helicopter to an altitude of eight thousand feet, from which vantage point Rainbow Valley's farms and plowed fields were spread out below them.

"Jake was different, Maya."

"You ever have a relationship with one before him?"

Shaking her head, Ana whispered, "No…just Roberto…and he was Peruvian."

"Well," Maya said, reaching out and rubbing her hand in a soothing motion across Ana's right shoulder, "don't expect too much, okay? They say a lot of things and never deliver on their promises. That's my unfortunate experience with them. They're afraid of responsibility and commitment to anything beyond a one-night stand."

Mouth quirking, Ana said, "Jake promised me nothing."

Raising her brows, Maya said, "Well, maybe he's a jaguar of different spots then, because those men up there are real good at lines and lies. I know—been there, done that." She glanced wryly at Ana for a moment. "I just don't want to see you hurt, Ana. You're a one-woman man. I saw that with you and Roberto. And it looks like you've fallen hard for this Jake Travers guy. I'm sorry. I really am. We'll keep you busy at the base and maybe that will lift some of your pain."

Yes, work always helped, Ana knew. "I won't be able to fly for five more weeks, Maya. I feel really awful about that…about the pressure it puts on you and the rest of our pilots."

Giving a derisive laugh, Maya said, "Don't worry about it. Consuelo is leaving in two weeks. She took care of getting the supplies for the base, and I don't have a replacement—yet. If you could go over to the mining side of the mountain, and work with her and take over her job, I'd be grateful. I've got a requisition in for a supply clerk, but the army, as usual, is dragging its feet. And I can't be without a supply clerk. You interested in that kind of collateral duty?"

Ana smiled gratefully at her commanding officer. "Sure. I'm pretty good with numbers. I'll help out any way I can."

Giving her a relieved look, Maya said, "Thanks…I was sweating this one. We're so undermanned all the time. And the damned CIA and Pentagon are strangling us with a budget that doesn't cover all our needs. I don't know what we're going to do…."

Ana heard the worry in Maya's husky tone. Over the last three years, they had literally carved the base out of nothing to fulfill Maya's vision, her belief that they and the other fifty army volunteers—all women—could make a difference in the drug trade in

Peru. Maya had found a huge cave inside a lava mountain fifty miles south of Agua Caliente, and for a year, Navy Seabees had helicoptered in all the necessary supplies to build the base. Ana knew from taking Apache helicopter training at Fort Rucker with Maya that the U.S. Army wanted all of them out from underfoot. Out of sight, out of mind was how the army wanted to deal with the scandal that had erupted while their class had undergone training on the Boeing Apache gunship.

Now Ana was worried as she looked out the window. The comforting tremble of the helicopter always soothed her anxiety. The green fields of Rainbow Valley flashed beneath them. She knew that the army would like to see Maya and her all-woman base die of monetary strangulation. Each year, they had cut Maya's budget more and more. The base was a spec ops, and money was usually thrown at such high priority items. But not at them. It was as if there were people in the army and the Pentagon who wanted to see them fail.

Well, Maya Stevenson wasn't going down without a fight, and Ana backed her a hundred percent. They ran shorthanded. The pressures were tremendous on all of them. They operated on a wartime footing every day of the year. So far, they'd been lucky and no one had been killed, but such a record couldn't hold forever, Ana knew. And with the pilots stretched to their physical limits, sleep deprivation the real enemy to all of them, it was only a matter of time.

Ana tucked the tissue away in the pocket of her jeans. If she could be of help to Maya as a clerk, then so be it. No job was too lowly or unimportant on the base, and every woman there was a team worker. There were no bruising egos at Black Jaguar Base. No, only a group of highly patriotic women who believed in their mission and in Maya Stevenson's vision.

Sniffing, Ana felt a little better, but she knew another storm of grief and loss would batter her later. Maybe working as a clerk and learning a new job would take her mind and heart off Jake—and her love for him. Because whether Ana liked it or not, she knew he would never return to her.

Chapter Ten

Jake stood in the living room of his parents' huge old two-story farmhouse, looking out the window. It was May and the trees were bursting with the first buds of spring. The last patches of snow had melted at the beginning of the month. *April showers bring May flowers,* he thought. In his hands was the *chalina*. Ana's *chalina*. The alpaca wool was soft and he stroked it tenderly with his fingers. Feeling it was like feeling her.

A sigh broke from him. As he scanned the farm, the lawn a sparkling green and yellow daffodils beginning to bloom along the concrete sidewalk leading from the house to the white picket fence, he tried to stop thinking about Ana. He saw his father walking to the big red barn to get his tractor. The land had dried out enough from the snow to begin the plowing and planting. Jake had wanted to help his father, but Tal had an appointment with her therapist in town and Jake wanted to drive her there.

The pleasant clink of dishes and pans being washed out in the kitchen by his mother soothed some of his inner restlessness. A day hadn't gone by in the three months since bringing Tal home to heal that he didn't think of Ana and their time with one another. His heart ached. He felt incomplete without her. That warm smile of hers lifted him, made him feel special and desired. Jake was sorry he hadn't made love to Ana, but in another way, he was glad he hadn't. From a point of integrity, he had respected the morals and values of her people, and her, by not taking her.

Looking down at the bright pink, red, orange and purple colors of Ana's rainbow *chalina,* he smiled sadly. Touching her scarf was as close as he was going to come to touching her.

"Jake?"

Hearing Tal's soft voice across the room, he partly turned, the scarf in his hands. Tal was standing there watching him through half-closed eyes. Since coming home, his sister had allowed her blond hair to grow. She had always worn it short, in a pixie style to show off the smooth oval planes of her face, but now it fell below her ears. As he searched her serious blue eyes, Jake realized that the physical trauma had healed. She was as pretty as ever. And she was learning to walk again, although she still had a slight limp. Her physical therapist was proud of her progress. But, the old Tal he knew and loved was gone. Or maybe *sub-*

merged was a better word to use, as the therapist had said. Because of the rape, she was now introverted, cautious, jumpy and hyperalert about every sound and everyone. Inwardly, Jake grieved daily for the changes in his younger sister.

"Yeah. What's up?" Jake quickly folded the scarf and set it on the back of the overstuffed couch. The living room was huge, with blond oak paneling that was nearly a hundred years old. Many generations of Travers had lived here and farmed the land before he and Tal had come along. Changing times and economics had stopped him and his sister from becoming farmers. Now Jake almost wished they had.

Tal watched him place the *chalina* on the sofa. "You were thinking of Ana?"

Shrugging, Jake stuffed his hands in the pockets of his jeans. "Yeah...I guess...."

One corner of her mouth hitched upward as she walked to where he stood. "You men," she teased gently. "Why is it so hard for you to admit you love someone?" She reached out and placed her arm around his broad shoulders, giving him a sisterly hug.

"I don't know if it's love," Jake muttered, avoiding her searching gaze.

"Don't you think you owe it to Ana and yourself to go back down to Peru and find out, then? There isn't a day that goes by that I don't see you sitting off by yourself, Jake, and thinking. And I know you're thinking about her." Tal eased her arm from around him and grazed the colorful *chalina* gently with her fingers. "It's beautiful," she murmured.

"Yeah..." he muttered, and cleared his throat,

wondering what his sister was up to. Ordinarily, Tal wasn't so talkative or sensitive about other people or their problems. She'd used to be, before the rape, but now she seemed to be diving headlong into a dark spiral that no one could pull her out of. The therapist had counseled the rest of the family that Tal had to go down into her wounding before she could arise from it.

Right now she was going through the five stages of grief; on any given day, and sometimes hourly, she would whipsaw between depression, tears and rage. It had taken Jake a long time to adjust to his sister's uneven emotional states. He tried to put himself in her shoes, and when he did, Jake was sure he'd be feeling a storm of emotions, too. Right now, as he looked at Tal, he realized she was in a very clear, stable state. There was even a hint of life in her dark blue eyes, and that gave him hope that she was getting better, even if it was at a snail's pace.

"Have you heard from Ana? I know you said you wrote her a couple of letters over the last month or two." Tal leaned against the couch and crossed her arms.

"No...not a word. My letters were returned to me, unopened." Why had he expected her to reply to the heartfelt words he'd penned so painstakingly in those letters? He couldn't promise Ana anything. They were a continent apart.

"Maybe she never got them. Mail to South America is often interrupted, lost or stolen."

"Yeah. Maybe the address was wrong or something...." How he wished. No, he felt Ana had gotten his letters and decided to not answer them. Instead, she'd handed them back to the post office and told the postmaster to send them back to him—unopened. Unanswered.

So Jake had remained with his sister. The therapist had told him that when she wanted to talk, he should listen. That he should be there for her. Not that Tal talked that much about what had happened, but Jake could see glimmers of change, good changes, in her this past month. She was slowly emerging from the trauma, and he felt a huge load lifting off his heart and shoulders. Everyone in the family was trying so hard to help Tal. On some days it worked, and on other days it was a painful hell for all of them to see what she was working to come to grips with. Jake still wanted to kill Rojas for what he'd done.

"Jake?"

"Yes?"

"I've made up my mind about something…and I hope you'll support me in my decision."

He looked over at her. Tal's face was serious. She was staring out the window, her lips compressed into a line that he recognized as stubbornness. Taking his hands out of his pockets, he said, "What decision?" He hadn't been aware that Tal was making any decisions about anything. His heart beat a little harder because he felt uneasy for no explainable reason.

"I just got off the phone with my therapist. I had a long talk with her." She slanted him a glance. "I'm going back down to my job in Peru. I want to go back to do what I went down there to do."

Shock bolted through him. Jake opened his mouth.

And then he snapped it shut. Ruthlessly examining her pensive features, her sad-looking eyes and the set of her lips, he rasped, "Are you crazy?" And then, just as quickly, he was sorry he'd said those words. Tal winced, as if struck.

"No, I'm not crazy," Tal told him tightly. She glared up at him. "I've given this a lot of thought for the last three months I've been home. I *need* to go back, Jake. I *have* to face it. Right now, I feel like a part of me is still down there. I need to reclaim the spirit Rojas stole from me, as silly as it might sound to you. I know I can do that only if I go back and live in those villages and do my job. That's part of my healing process, whether you think it is or not."

Gulping, Jake stared at her. "But…your therapist…what did she say?" He held out his hand toward her.

"She's backing me in my decision," Tal told him quietly. She unlocked her arms and ran her slender fingers through her ruffled blond hair. "I'm scared, but I have to do this, Jake. And that's why I'm telling you first about the idea."

"But," he sputtered, "the Wiraqocha Foundation. Do they want you to go back?"

"Sure…they have a five-year contract with me."

"And they talked you into going back down there? Back to Rojas's turf?" His mind spun. Jake didn't know if Rojas was dead or alive. He assumed it was the latter. Tal would be working in villages within his little drug fiefdom. Tal would be once again in danger's path.

"No. They had nothing to do with this decision,

Jake. I called them. They didn't call me. And yes, they'd like to have me come back down to Peru. Those villages still need wells. You saw the children, how cute they are. How loving. Can you imagine sixty percent of them dying by age ten just because they can't get a good, safe water supply? Can you?'' Her blue gaze drilled into his eyes.

"I understand, but I don't agree with what you're going to do,'' he growled. "I don't think you're emotionally strong enough yet to handle it.''

She gave him a one-shouldered shrug. "Since when did a Travers hide from the dragon? You sure haven't. Look at you—you're an army ranger.''

"I was,'' Jake said heavily. "That's done. I can't go back.''

Tal gave him a gentle look. "I was thinking, Jake…about contacting Morgan Trayhern. I know he has a service, bodyguards, I think. What do you think if I ask him to send someone along down there, to stay with me? Guard me? It would be temporary, of course…maybe two or three months until I can get my feet under me…''

He saw Tal's brow wrinkle, and noted the searching look in her wide blue eyes. His heart was thudding hard. Ana's face loomed before him. How badly Jake wanted to see her. And he realized that Tal was lifting the responsibility from him to go down there with her. She was honoring the fact that he had a life to live, too, and she wasn't going to ask him to come with her. His mind raced. If he went down to guard Tal, he would not be able to see Ana. No, he'd have to remain by his sister's side at all times, vigilant and alert. He couldn't just take off when he wanted to, to go visit Ana. That would leave Tal wide-open and vulnerable, and he wouldn't do that to his healing sibling.

Rubbing his jaw, he said, "Yeah…that might work. I like the idea of you having a merc at your side."

"I thought you might." She managed a crooked smile. "Could you call Mr. Trayhern? I don't know what something like this costs. I've got some stocks and mutual funds I could sell to pay for a bodyguard."

Jake held up his hand. "Let me talk to him, okay? I know he has a fund for people like us who aren't rich or famous, to pay for his services."

Reaching out, Tal gripped his hand. "Thanks for being here for me, Jake. I love you so much."

Squeezing her hand gently, Jake moved over to Tal and gave her a brief hug. Even he, her brother, could feel Tal retreat when he touched her. Oh, it wasn't really obvious, but Jake could feel her cringing inwardly. He was a man, after all, and a man had wounded her deeply. Jake tried to understand that and tried not to take Tal's retreat from him personally. "Let me call him. Let's see what he says," he whispered as he released her.

Later that night, after a dinner of fried chicken, peas slathered with butter, and mashed potatoes, Jake sat with his family around the kitchen table. His parents, both in their fifties, kept giving him and Tal questioning looks. They knew something was up. Jake cleared his throat and began.

"Mom, Dad, Tal has made up her mind to go back down to Peru." He saw the shock and worry in their eyes. Holding up his hands, he added quickly, "But she's going to have an escort, a mercenary who will be with her twenty-four hours a day. Morgan Trayhern is doing this gratis for Tal...for us. The mercenary Mr. Trayhern has chosen will be with Tal for however long she needs him."

"But," Susan Travers said as she reached out and gripped her daughter's hand, "what about Rojas?"

"Mom," Tal said, "he's still down there. Mr. Trayhern said in the after-action report he received from Lieutenant Cortina that Rojas was still in business."

"That means," Roy Travers said heavily, his gray brows drawing downward, "that you're still in danger, honey."

Jake held up his hands. "I've got a plan...one that I think will work for all of us." He gave Tal a hopeful look. "The merc Morgan has assigned has a lot of years in the business and he's an ex-Navy SEAL. That's as good as it gets. The man knows his stuff and he'll protect Tal or die trying." He managed a slight smile. "And I'll be traveling back down with her."

Tal gasped. "You will?"

Jake nodded. "Yeah, but I've got a dual reason for it, as you know. I need to find out about Ana and myself. If she doesn't want to pursue a relationship with me, well, I'll hang around for a month or two with you until my savings account runs out, and then I'll have to come back up here and find a job in order to live."

Gasping, Tal clasped her hands, joy in her eyes. "Oh, Jake! That's wonderful! Does Ana know you're coming?"

Shaking his head, he muttered, "No. I asked Morgan Trayhern how to contact that spec ops place she works out of, and he gave me some information. I'll track her down that way."

"And if she does want a relationship with you?" his mother asked gently. "What then, Son?"

Holding his mother's watery blue gaze, framed by her gray-and-black hair, he said, "I don't know, Mom. It will be one step at a time. I don't have a job and I'll have to get one. I have no idea where or how.... There's a lot of complexity to the situation and I don't have answers right now. Everything depends upon Ana...."

"Well," Roy said, picking up his coffee cup between his spare, weathered hands, "what if it does work between you and Ana?"

"Then," Jake said, giving Tal a warm look, "I can be nearby. I can go visit Tal maybe once a week, maybe on weekends, and just see how she's doing. Maybe be there to support her, or just let her talk. Whatever she needs…"

Tears glimmered in Tal's eyes. "Oh, Jake, this is such a wonderful idea! I'm so glad you're coming back with me!"

Jake nodded. He was scared to death. How would Ana receive him? Or would she? Ana probably thought he'd forgotten her. Forgotten their warm, life-giving kisses, their long, searching talks.

"Well," Susan whispered, blotting her eyes and giving her husband a warm look, "you kids have a plan. And I think it's a good one. We'll worry for you, honey." She took her daughter's hand and squeezed it. "I know you'll have a bodyguard, but we'll still worry."

Tal nodded. "I'm not sitting here and telling you I feel great about my decision, Mom and Dad. But I know in my heart and gut that I've got to *face* that monster, face the situation in order to be released from it once and for all. I'm scared, but I'm going forward." She gave Jake a grateful glance. "And having Jake down there, even for a little while, will make me feel better, too."

Jake sat there, his heart pounding like a sledgehammer in his chest. He was worried for Tal. They would meet the mercenary down in Peru, at Agua Caliente. Apparently the man that Morgan Trayhern had in mind was a hard-as-nails ex-SEAL officer who was in the midst of returning from a harrowing mission over in Serbia. He would touch base with Morgan and then hop another flight out for Peru. The paperwork and airline tickets were already in motion. Jake had the name of the man: Sloan Griffin.

More than anything, Jake tried to wrestle with his own feelings about Ana. What she meant to him. How would she react to seeing him again? Would Ana be angry? Maybe. Disappointed that he'd showed up like a bad penny in her life again? Probably. Rubbing his eyes tiredly, Jake admitted to himself that he was scared. He loved Ana. And he knew it. Did she love him, though? So many questions, and no answers…and the only way he'd find out was by showing up at that hidden base deep in the Peruvian jungle.

"Maya? You wanted to see me?" Ana held her helmet in her left fingers by the chin strap. It was early evening and she'd just come off a mission and was exhausted.

Her C.O. was hard at work in her tiny, cramped office in the two-story headquarters building within the cave. She looked up, a slight smile on her full mouth as she set her pen aside. "Yes, Ana. How'd the mission go? Did you make those two civilian helos turn back from the Bolivian border?"

Ana nodded and stepped inside the office. She ran her fingers through her mussed hair. While on the flight roster for a twenty-four-hour period, she always braided her hair into one thick strand so it was out of the way. "Yes, we turned them back."

"Faro Valentino's Russian mercenaries?"

"Yes. We got a visual on them. Same merc pilots posing as civilian pilots." Ana grinned a little. "Can't shoot 'em out of the sky, but we can turn them back by staring them down with our missiles, rockets and cannon on board the Apache."

"It's a deterrent," Maya agreed. She folded her hands on her paper-strewn desk. "I've got one helluva surprise for you. Are you prepared for it?"

Puzzled, Ana shrugged. "Surprise? A good one, I hope?"

With a shrug, Maya murmured, "I don't know…
It's up to you to decide that."

Frowning, Ana said, "My parents? Are they
okay?" They lived in Rainbow Valley, and ever since
the run-in with Rojas, Ana had been fearful for them.
If Rojas ever found out she was one of the people
that had sprung Tal Travers, he would go after them
and kill them. That was what drug lords did—they
always got even with the offending party by murder-
ing their whole family. She'd had some nightmares
about that off and on in the last three months since
Tal had left Peru.

Holding up her hand, Maya said, "Whoa…good
news, I think. Your parents are fine. Go to your office,
Ana. There's someone waiting there to see you." And
she grinned warmly up at her.

Stymied, Ana said, "Who?" Who would visit her
at their hidden base? No one that she knew. The look
on Maya's face reminded her of a jaguar that had
caught its quarry and was quite pleased with herself.
And the indulgent look on her C.O.'s features only
deepened her confusion.

Waving her hand, Maya said, "Go find out, Ana.
If we get lucky, you won't have any more missions
tonight."

Turning, Ana moved wearily out into the narrow
hall. Most of the offices had their doors open, which
was Maya's policy. And most of the clerks had left
for the day, except a few who had night duty. Frowning, Ana saw that the door to her office was closed,
which was unusual. She always left it open. She
twisted the knob, opened it and pushed it aside.

"Jake!"

Jake shot out of the chair he'd been sitting in. Ana's voice echoed oddly through the small room. He saw the shock in her face and the pain that came instantly to her cinnamon eyes.

"Ana?" His voice was off-key. He'd purposely worn the *chalina* around his neck, the ends of it hanging down across his bright red polo shirt. How beautiful she looked to him. She wore the one-piece black flight suit that lovingly outlined her tall, proud form. From it and the darkness beneath her eyes, he knew the mission she'd flown had been long and intense.

"W-what are you doing here?"

He slowly approached her. He ached to kiss her. He saw the shock and fear and joy in her eyes. Was she glad to see him? Jake wasn't sure. "Tal is back down here," he told her quietly. "I came with her."

"What?" Ana gasped. "Tal's back here? So soon after…after what happened to her?"

"I know it's crazy," Jake said as he halted a good two feet away from her, "but she wants to face her personal demons. I couldn't let her come down alone. She's got a merc bodyguard who will be with her all the time, but I didn't want her down here by herself…. At least…for a couple of months, until I can make sure she's going to be okay."

"But," Ana whispered, her heart beating hard in her breast, "Rojas is still around! If he finds out she's back, he'll swear blood vengeance against her." Ana searched his dark face and saw exhaustion in Jake's eyes. But she also saw longing there, too—for her. When her gaze fell to the *chalina,* she didn't know what to say, so she stood there feeling helpless beneath his hungry scrutiny. Jake was back here because of Tal. Not her. Wrestling with that painful realization, Ana wondered why he was wearing her *chalina,* then. To give it back to her? Probably. Grief shattered her. Her love for Jake had not died quietly—had not died at all. No, since he'd left, she'd grieved deeply. There wasn't a day that went by that Ana didn't think of him, or what might have been between them if things had been different.

"I know he will," Jake admitted heavily. Holding out his hand toward her, he got up the courage to tell her why he was here at the base to see her. "Listen, I tried to write to you...three letters...and they were all returned to me as undeliverable."

Ana's eyes widened. "You did? You wrote to me?" Had he been following tradition by writing her the all-important letters, just as her father had to her mother? Her heart bounded hard. How badly she wanted to take those last steps and simply throw her arms around Jake and kiss him senseless. She saw the darkness in his eyes. By the way he moved his mouth, she knew he was nervous.

"Yeah..." Jake dug into his pocket and pulled out the badly wrinkled letters. "Did they get here? Did you see them?"

Confused, she stared at them as he held them in his hand, and then up into his unfathomable, dark eyes. "Why, no...I've never seen them...."

His heart pounded fiercely in his chest. His hopes rose with his fear. "I see.... Well, here—I want you to have them. So read them, to see if... Well, you need to read them, Ana. Please?'' He hesitantly offered them to her.

Staring at the dog-eared letters, and then up at Jake again, Ana slowly reached out. Their fingertips met. Heat rushed up Ana's arm as she broke the contact. ''I—I just got back from a mission, Jake. I'm on duty for twenty-four hours....''

''I know you've got duty tonight. You have a lot of things going on right now. Maybe, when you're done with your shift, you could read them and get back to me?''

Swallowing hard, Ana closed the door. She set her helmet down on her desk behind Jake. ''I'll read them now. I don't have a flight unless the warning bells ring. Please...sit down?'' She gestured to a chair near the desk.

Jake sat with hope filling his chest. He watched as Ana took the chair behind the desk. It creaked loudly in protest. His heart hurt. How would she react to them? To sit here and watch her was agony. Jake didn't know how he was going to handle Ana's reactions. They were love letters. Letters telling of his love for her...and asking whether or not she would reciprocate. They were long, painfully penned letters. He wasn't a letter writer and had struggled ungodly hours finding the right words and phrases to describe what lay in his heart for Ana. The first envelope she opened up had six blue-lined sheets of tablet-size paper in it, and there was a lot to read, since he'd used the front and back of each sheet. He had poured his heart out to her in those letters and said the things he hadn't had the guts to say to her face.

As he sat there tensely, his fists on his thighs, Jake watched every nuance of expression on Ana's face as she slowly read each page. What would she say? Closing his eyes, exhaustion pulling at him, Jake knew his life—the life he dreamed of every night since he'd left Ana—was about to be decided.

Ana stole a look at Jake's dark, exhausted features as she finished the first letter. Her hands shook as she delicately refolded it and slid it back into the envelope. She saw hope burning in his eyes. Pain and joy savaged her. The silence thickened. Holding the envelope tenderly, Ana closed her eyes for a moment.

"You wrote this letter a week after you left here?"

"Yes," Jake rasped. "Because I hadn't heard from you, I wrote a second one." He pointed to where it sat on the desk in front of her. His voice trembled with barely checked emotion. "Another month rolled by and I was desperate, Ana. The other two, I guess, were being held in the Agua Caliente post office. I wrote a third one hoping you'd received the first two." Mouth quirking, Jake whispered, "I got all three of them back in late May, unopened. Undelivered." He saw the hurt burning in her eyes.

"I'm sorry, Ana. I tried...really tried to contact you."

Wiping her eyes with her fingers, Ana's voice cracked. "I thought...I thought you'd walked out of my life forever, Jake."

Hanging his head, he rasped, "I'm sure it seemed that way." When Ana looked at him, he mustered a faint smile. "But you gotta admit, trying to send letters to a spec ops base that's not supposed to exist…well, I think the Peruvian post office tried, but they didn't know where you were at, either.''

Ana slowly rose. ''You're right. What's important to me is that you tried.'' She held out the envelope as she approached him. Kneeling down in front of him, Ana set it aside and placed her hands over his. ''In the letter, you said you loved me.'' Her heart thrashed in her chest as her gaze dug into his hooded eyes. ''Is that true, Jake? Did you?'' She held her breath, unable to prepare herself for his answer.

Reaching out, Jake tenderly slid his hands around her face. ''Did? I still do, Ana. I *never* stopped loving you.'' He met and held her tearful eyes. ''I don't know when or how it happened. All I know is it did. At the time, neither of us could talk about it. Hell, for all I know, Ana, my love for you is one-sided. I could be down here on a wild-goose chase. But I had to find out. I have to know….''

Sniffing, Ana closed her eyes and simply absorbed his warmth and strength from the hands that framed her face. ''I gave you my *chalina,* didn't I, Jake?''

''Yes…yes, you did….''

Opening her eyes, Ana saw the tenderness burning in his. ''When a Quechua woman gives a man her *chalina,* she's serious. I gave you mine. And I'm still serious about you. I love you. I never stopped loving you, either….''

Chapter Eleven

Just as Jake leaned down to capture Ana's lips, he heard a sharp, clanging bell reverberating loudly throughout the building. Ana gasped. She leaped to her feet. "What? What's wrong?" Jake demanded, quickly standing. He saw Ana's expression change to one of sharpened focus, her brows drawing downward.

"It's the warning bell, Jake." She hurried over and grabbed her helmet. Jerking the door open, Ana turned. "I'm on duty. That's the call for me to get to the Apache. They've spotted drug runners in our vicinity and we've got to intercept. I'm sorry...I've got to go. Wait for me?"

He opened his mouth to speak, but she was gone, running down the hall toward the exit. Jake saw several other on-duty crew race past Ana's door. Standing in the doorway, Jake saw another woman pilot, dressed in a black uniform like Ana's, rush past him. Her face was set, too, just as Ana's had been. Women in combat. Suddenly, it was a reality for him.

His heart pounded with fear—for Ana. This was the first time he'd gotten a taste of her life as a U.S. Army pilot. He saw Captain Stevenson walk out of her office and stand in the hallway. Her darkened emerald gaze settled on him.

The clanging of the bell stopped. Jake turned to her. He'd met her earlier when he'd landed at the base complex. She had been down at the helo pad when the civilian helicopter had dropped him off.

"Sorry you couldn't have some quality time with Ana," she told him as she walked up, her hands on her hips.

"Does this happen often?"

Maya laughed sharply. "All the time. Come on, follow me. You want to see what we do around here?"

Jake did. He followed her along the hall and down two flights of metal stairs, his worry for Ana gnawing at him. As they stepped out of the building onto the black lava floor of the huge cave complex, he saw two Apache helicopters out on the lip, outside the cave, their rotors whirling in preparation for takeoff.

As Jake and Maya walked toward them, the wind kicked up by the rotors started to pummel them. Jake kept his hand over his eyes. Crews were scurrying around, then backing off as the first Apache lifted into a hover.

"Ana is piloting that one," Maya said, pointing to it. "She's commander of the flight." Halting just inside the cave, Maya glanced over at Jake. "From the look on your face, Mr. Travers, I'd guess you really didn't understand what Ana does here."

"I had an idea…. Ana didn't speak much about it to me…." Jake watched with dread and fascination as Ana approached a huge opening in the lava wall. The hole was just large enough to allow one helicopter at a time to fly through it—very carefully. One wrong move, and he knew those rotor blades would nick either side of it and the chopper would crash.

After the second Apache moved through the hole in the wall, the antique black Cobra from the Vietnam era followed. Once the choppers were outside the thick, protective wall, Jake couldn't hear the whapping of the blades as well. Very soon, the sounds faded completely. He looked over at Maya, who, at six feet tall, was nearly eye level with him. Her black hair was loose about her shoulders, almost covering her breasts. The look on her face was one of concern.

"How often does this happen? The bell going off?"

Maya moved toward the lip, which was now clear of aircraft. The crews for the three birds were clearing away the chalk blocks and already preparing the landing pads for the helos' return.

"A number of times every day." She walked out on the lip, where the early evening sunlight was hazy because of the ever-present fog. "Ana will intercept Faro Valentino's pilots probably twenty miles inside the Peruvian border. Valentino is a big-time drug lord who's got a fleet of helicopters—Russian military as well as civilian ones from other countries—that he uses to try and ferry cocaine across the border to Bolivia."

"And Ana is going to stop Valentino now?" Jake's heart beat hard in his chest.

"Yes, Mr. Travers, she will. That's her job here— to stop the coke shipments." Maya pointed toward the east. "You see, Bolivia won't stop the shipments. They don't have the money, the trained personnel, so they just let the coke come in from Peru without putting up any resistance. It's flown out of Bolivia on private airlines owned by the drug lords, to be sent all over the world." Her voice lowered. "Our job is to stop it at the Peruvian border, turn it around and cause havoc with Valentino's distribution plans."

"But," Jake said, "you mentioned Russian military helicopters? Those Kamov Black Shark's, right?"

She gave him an amused look. "Yeah, the one that nearly killed all of you several months ago. That's the one."

And Ana was going to face that lethal helicopter. Jake reminded himself that she was a trained gunship pilot; she knew what she was doing. But his mouth went a little dry and he croaked, "Has Ana ever been shot down?"

Maya shook her head. "No. But she crash-landed once, and she's been shot at plenty, just as all of us here have. It's part of our business." Maya studied Jake. "Ana said you were an officer in the army. A ranger. Is that right?"

"I was, yes. I recently resigned my commission."

"And your sister—Talia, I think her name was, if my memory serves me—how is she doing? Ana said she was the most severely wounded when the Kamov attacked all of you."

Grimacing, Jake turned to her. He found Maya easy to speak to. Ana had made her C.O. out to be a legend, someone who almost walked on water. Yet he found Maya beautiful, pragmatic and caring. Around them, the women crews were working constantly; the base was a beehive of activity. "My sister," he said in a strained tone, "is back down here after only three months recuperation."

Maya's brows moved upward. "Down *here?* After what happened to her?"

"Yes, and back at the same village where she was kidnapped. She's determined to get those wells sunk so the people have a safe water supply."

Maya shook her head. "You've got one tough, stubborn sister then. I honor her courage. You know Rojas is still on the loose over in Rainbow Valley?"

"Yes…I do know that. The people who helped me rescue her, Perseus, have good intel on him and his whereabouts."

Lips tightening, Maya muttered, "That little bastard is still causing trouble in the valley. He's in cahoots with Faro now, and is under his protection. Faro's using civilian helos to fly into that hill villa of Rojas's to pick up cocaine." Shaking her head, Maya added grimly, "I hope your sister has some protection. Is that why you're here?"

"Yes and no," Jake admitted. "Morgan Trayhern,

who owns Perseus, sent an ex-Navy SEAL down to be her bodyguard. His name is Sloan Griffin.''

''That's good,'' Maya said, relief in her voice. ''Because when Rojas finds out she's back, his *mano a mano* pride will kick in and I'm sure he'll try to seek revenge against her.''

Alarmed, Jake stood there in the slanting sunlight, the humid equatorial heat still intense after the long day. Maya, in comparison, looked cool, without a bead of sweat on her. Wiping his perspiring brow, he said, ''I'll let them know right away. Thanks for telling me.''

Nodding, Maya gestured for him to follow her back into the cave. ''Ana is going to be gone a number of hours. What are your plans, Mr. Travers?''

''Call me Jake if you want, Captain Stevenson.''

''Okay…Jake.'' She headed back toward the building in the center of the cave complex. ''Have you eaten?''

''No, I haven't.''

''You look like hell warmed over. Musta taken the red-eye to get down here, eh? Come with me. We'll feed you at the mess and then find you a place to sleep it off.''

''Captain…I didn't mean for you to go to all this trouble. I can see how busy you are….''

Maya looked over at him, a slight grin playing at the corners of her mouth. ''Ana says you're special to her. Frankly speaking, she's been in a deep depression since Roberto died. When you showed up in her life she began to live again, Jake. I'm sure it's because of you…and whatever is going on between

the two of you.'' Maya headed off to the left toward
a Quonset hut with a large red sign that said Mess.
Her emerald eyes sparkled as she held his gaze. ''I
don't have any spare pilots, Jake. I need every woman
pilot I have in good health physically, mentally and
emotionally. Ana was doing a helluva lot better when
she came back from that little hike with you than I've
seen her in a long time.'' Gripping his arm, she
opened the door to the mess and ushered him into it.
''By taking care of you, I'm taking care of Ana.''
And she smiled.

Jake found himself in a long hall with several rows
of wooden picnic tables. About fifteen crew women
were sitting at various tables. It was just past supper-
time. On the left was the mess line. Maya handed him
an aluminum tray and they went through the line,
where the cook served them whatever they wanted
from various cooking pans.

Sitting down at an empty table near the corrugated
aluminum wall of the Quonset hut, Jake began to eat
hungrily. The fare was fresh and tasty, and there was
a lot of it. Maya, who sat opposite him, ate very little.
She seemed preoccupied and picked at her food. A
number of times, office clerks would spot her from
the door and hurry over with papers in hand. They
would whisper in her ear and she'd rapidly scribble
her signature on the papers, or give them orders to
carry out. Jake knew the responsibilities on Maya's
shoulders were many. Although very young—she was
probably around twenty-five or twenty-six years
old—she seemed very mature for her age.

"Looks like peace and quiet are hard to come by," Jake noted, drinking his coffee.

With a chuckle, Maya nodded. "We're on wartime footing around here. There's no rest for the wicked, as they say." Her eyes glinted as she looked up at him. "And I guess we're a pretty wicked lot because we're up to our butts in alligators around here all the time."

Shaking his head, Jake said, "Ana said that your vision for this base and what you're all doing here is making a big difference. I'd say you're stopping the wicked." He grinned a little at her dry humor. He liked Maya Stevenson a lot. She was a good leader, in Jake's eyes. The warmth her people had for her was obvious. Maya had earned that respect from them the hard way: by being an excellent manager of people. Not all C.O.s were good leaders or managers, and she seemed to be both.

Maya pushed her partly eaten food aside and wrapped her hands around the thick white ceramic mug that held her steaming coffee. "That's probably more accurate." Her eyes narrowed on him. "So, what're your intentions toward Ana? Why are you back here if your sister has a big, bad guard dog with her? We're a little out of your way, so I know there's more here than meets the eye."

Shocked by her point-blank question, Jake stared at her a moment. Ana had said Maya shot from the hip. She was right. Setting his own mug down on the table, he decided to be just as brutally frank and honest with her. "If I can get some time with Ana, I want to see how she feels about me…about us, maybe. I'm not sure what her answer will be, though.''

"How do you feel toward her?'' Maya demanded.

Jake's mouth curved slightly. More point-blank questions. Well, Ana had warned him about Maya's methods. "I love her.''

"Does she love you?''

"She's told me she does.''

Maya scowled. "So you love one another. What now?''

Shrugging, Jake said, "I don't really know, Captain. I know Ana wants to stay here. I wouldn't think of asking her to leave. This is her life. She loves what she does.''

"So,'' Maya said, lifting the cup to her lips, "what are *you* going to do?''

"That's the question,'' Jake answered. "I don't think there's much call for an ex-army ranger down in Agua Caliente, the closest town to your base, is there?''

Grinning sourly, Maya sipped her coffee. Her eyes were speculative. "No, there isn't….''

"Well,'' Jake said, "if Ana loves me, I'll figure out something. I know she's Quechua by birth, and I want to do things the right way according to the customs of her people.''

"Good.'' Maya smiled a little. A tight smile. "You're surprising me, Jake. Most *norteamericano* males aren't worth the powder to blow them up.''

Again, Jake just stared at her in shock. He saw the wry amusement dancing in her thoughtful eyes. "I assume you're speaking from experience, and—'' he looked around the mess hall ''—that's why you have all women here at this base, and no men. Right?''

''You could say that. Based upon my experiences with the U.S. Army up at Fort Rucker, Alabama, I decided women were a lot more team-oriented and would pull together in the same direction. We don't have those little ego temper tantrums that men are given to from time to time.'' She held his look, her mouth compressed, as if daring him to refute her words.

Jake wouldn't do it. ''You're right,'' he admitted. ''Teamwork is everything in something like this.''

''You know teamwork from being a ranger.''

Nodding, he smiled a little. ''There's no room for egotistical John Wayne types in our ranks. We live or die together—as a team.''

''I like your attitude, Jake.'' Maya tapped her fingers on the table for a moment. ''I've got an idea…but a lot of things need to happen before and if it's put into place.'' She cocked her head and studied him intently. ''You aren't like most of the army guys I've had the sad occasion to lock horns with. I like your spirit and your sense of teamwork. If things work out between you and Ana, I might have a part-time job for you, if you're interested.''

His brows rose in surprise. ''A job? Here?''

''Not exactly here,'' Maya said. ''You landed on the other side of this ten-thousand-foot, loaf-shaped mountain and it is an old mining quarry. We get all our supplies flown in by civilian helicopters to that mine. The helos are really CIA owned and operated, but no one knows that. To outsiders and *touristas,* it looks like the mining company is up and running, so supplies going to it don't raise suspicions. I also have company housing over there, where everyone lives when off duty. There are some nice little plots of land down below, near the housing. A lot of good, fertile land. I've been looking for someone to help do some serious farming for us. We're always short on food supplies, especially fresh vegetables and fruit. It can grow here year-round. Ana said you were a farmer. Maybe I can hire you five days a week—three days working as supply officer and the other two overseeing our farming efforts.''

Jake was impressed. ''When I was flown in on the mining side, I was taken by a golf cart through a naturally occurring lava tube, eight feet high and ten feet wide, that extends from the mine operation back into this mountain.''

Maya finished off her coffee and set the mug aside. ''When the Navy Seabees came, they blasted out a tunnel from our cave facility to it. We run electric golf carts back and forth between them, and get our supplies, our weapons and other munitions into the cave to load onto our Apaches. Out of sight, out of mind, as they say.'' She smiled hugely, like a jaguar who had devoured a satisfying meal.

''So, what job do you think I can do for you, Captain, if things work out between Ana and me?''

Leaning forward, Maya rested her elbows on the table and gave him a frank look. ''Ana is doubling her collateral duty around here because I lost my supply officer three months ago. Her original task was housing. When she busted her ribs, she agreed to

learn the supply end of our trade while she couldn't
fly. So for three months the slot was filled by her.
Since she came back to flight duty, I still haven't been
able to fill the billet. The army is saying the paperwork I sent to them is lost. What's really happening
is they're choke-holding us and want to see this spec
ops die. By slowing down my requests for personnel,
they hurt us down here, and they know that. I'll be
damned if I'm quitting this base or our mission for
them. Ana's been juggling supply with housing demands ever since, and I'm anxious to get that off her
back. It's just too much for one person to handle, and
I can't be without a supply officer."

"I see." Jake shook his head. "Supply is a demanding job. I don't see how Ana is doing it all." It
worried him that she was probably taking sleep time
to do the extra work. And sleep deprivation was a
killer, especially if she had to be alert and on top of
things in the air with the Kamovs threatening them
constantly.

"Yes," Maya said heavily, "it is." She opened her
hand. "Now, I can't pay you much, but I think you
could do the job because you're ex-military. You understand how the army operates, too, since you're
from that branch of the service. My budget is tight,
but I could give you the job, and a place to live over
on the mining side with Ana."

Jake's heart leaped at her offer. "I'd like to stay in
the military, and maybe this would be the way to
continue it," he murmured.

"Supply isn't exactly as exciting as being a
ranger," Maya said, probing him mercilessly with her

eyes. "I don't want to offer you a job you're not going to be passionate about."

Turning the cup slowly around in his large hands, Jake said softly, "I can be happy anywhere, doing anything, Captain, if I have Ana's love. And having a house and a little plot of land to farm...well, that's my dream come true."

After measuring him for a while in silence, Maya sighed. "Okay...let me know how things turn out." She rose from the table and rapped her knuckles on the wood. "When Ana returns, I'm pulling her off the duty roster. I'll have one of my standby pilots take the rest of her twenty-four-hour tour. I suggest you take the civilian helicopter on the mining side to Agua Caliente, where you two can have some uninterrupted, quality time with one another. I'll have my assistant reserve a room for you at Gringo Bill's Hostel where we usually put our personnel who go on R and R." Maya smiled a little. "Okay with you?"

Jake nodded. "Sounds good. Thanks, Captain Stevenson—for everything."

Her eyes glittered. "Don't mistake my intentions, Jake. I'd like to see you two get together because I'm in desperate need of a supply officer. And someone who knows farming."

Laughing softly, Jake watched her stride away. Maya spoke to every person in the mess hall before she left. She was a charismatic leader, for each woman responded enthusiastically to her attention, as if she was showering them with sunlight. Maya made him feel special, too. Jake sat there a long time, nursing his coffee, thinking about what she'd said. Captain Stevenson was giving him an incredible opportunity. He would be where Ana was based. They would have a small company house to live in. He would have a job. Jake shook his head, stunned and mystified by how life could kink and unkink, and opportunities could literally materialize out of the ethers far beyond his imagination.

Right now, though, all he wanted was for Ana to return safe and sound to him so they could talk…and he could find out how they stood with one another. She had said she loved him. He'd seen it in her wide, tearful cinnamon eyes. He clung to her words and the look she'd given him. Now, if only Ana would come back to him safely… Worried about the Kamovs, Jake reminded himself bitterly that every day Ana flew, the possibility of her being killed would be there staring at him. He compressed his mouth, knowing now as never before what the wives of men in combat went through. It was pure, raw hell. And there was no escape from it.

Ana was walking away from her Apache with her copilot, Vickey Maybrey, when she spotted Jake coming out to meet her. Instantly, her heart rate accelerated. She clung to his warm, welcoming blue gaze. There was a cockeyed smile on his face. Something was going on. She could see it in his eyes as he approached her. Ana halted and introduced her copilot to Jake. They shook hands and Vickey politely excused herself.

"How did the mission go?" Jake asked, standing

with his hands in his pockets, because if he didn't, he'd be reaching out for Ana.

She shrugged tiredly and fell into step with him as they walked back into the cave facility. "Same old stuff. We locate them, we face them down, they turn around and go back into Peru."

"No shots were fired?"

"No. They're in civilian helicopters. All we do is intercept and detour at that point." Ana looked up at him. Jake seemed very relaxed compared to their first meeting. She wondered what the smile on his face was about.

"And Kamovs? Did you see any?"

Raising her brows, Ana whispered fervently, "No, thank goodness."

"What do you have to do now?"

"Go into HQ, to my office, and fill out two flight reports. And then I'm still on duty for another twelve hours. After that—"

"Captain Stevenson is pulling you off the mission roster, Ana." He held her widening eyes. "She's giving us some time away from the base. How'd you like to fly into Agua Caliente and stay at Gringo Bill's Hostel with me as soon as you're done with those reports?" His heart pounded strongly in his chest as he saw her eyes grow warm and tender.

"Ohh...how wonderful of Maya..." Ana reached out and briefly touched his arm in reaction. "That's wonderful, Jake! What a great surprise!"

"You'll go with me then?" There was hope and terror in his voice. He saw her expression soften, heard her voice become husky with feeling.

"Of course I will." Ana reached out and ran her fingers lightly down the *chalina* he wore around his neck. "Come on up. You can sit quietly in my office while I get the paperwork out of the way, and then I'll run over to my room and change into civvies. We can take one of the golf carts through the tunnel to the mining side and hitch a ride to Agua Caliente from there."

Her eyes were sparkling with joy. Jake found himself walking on air as they climbed the two flights of stairs to her office. Trying to contain the hope that burned in his chest, Jake found himself starved for Ana's every look and gesture. Whether she was lifting her slender fingers to push away a dark strand of hair from her cheek, or to smooth locks in disarray from wearing her helmet, each movement filled him with love and hunger for her.

In her office, which was spare and tiny, Jake saw the massive amounts of paperwork heaped like leaning towers of Pisa in wire baskets on either side of her desk. A number of other piles were also begging for attention, but she ignored them as she set her helmet on a cabinet and hurried to sit behind her military-issue, green metal desk.

Sitting down in turn, Jake looked at the cream-colored walls. The window behind her had white venetian blinds across it. Dull light shone through from the cave entrance in the distance. The only living things on her desk were several orchid spikes loaded with white blossoms with purple lips. They shouted of beauty and life.

As he watched Ana quickly work on the mission

reports, her head down, pen in hand, a powerful love for her moved through Jake. She was so responsible, for someone so young. Brave and courageous, too. Knowing what he knew of her, he could see she was an extraordinary woman. Jake could hear the murmur of women's voices outside in the hall. All the doors in the building were open. Clerks worked intently at their jobs. Sometimes Jake heard softened laughter. He'd been in enough HQs to know that this one was a happy one. But then, they had one helluva commanding officer: Maya Stevenson.

"There…" Ana murmured finally, standing up. She flashed him an eager smile. "Done! Let me run this down the hall to the clerk's office. I also want to poke my head into Maya's office and thank her. I need to find out if I've got twenty-four hours leave or what."

"Okay," Jake said, standing. "I'll wait here."

Ana gave him a tender smile and rushed out of her office. Jake felt his patience thinning. How badly he wanted to simply have time to sit and talk to Ana. And even though Captain Stevenson had told him up front that she was giving Ana time alone with him because she was hoping that he'd come to work for her, Jake felt he knew better. Maya Stevenson might be a hard-nosed, practical C.O., but he also heard the softness in her voice when she'd talked about Ana, her depression and how she'd changed since meeting him. More than anything, Jake knew, Maya wanted Ana happy. She was the type of C.O. who knew that if her people were happy, they were more productive at their jobs—and they stayed alive, too.

Ana rushed back in, breathless. Her eyes were shining with happiness. She gripped his hand. "Maya is giving us forty-eight hours, Jake! I'm in shock! Isn't that wonderful?" She leaned forward and impulsively pressed her lips to his.

Jake groaned. Caught off guard, he started to lift his arms and haul Ana into them, but just as quickly, the kiss was over and she was hurrying to the cabinet to pick up her helmet.

"I'll be right back! I've got to change into *tourista* clothes so I don't raise any suspicions over there in Agua Caliente." Giving him a careless smile, Ana reached out and touched his lips with her fingertips. "I love you, Jake Travers. Don't you move!"

Chapter Twelve

Ana quietly closed the door of their room at the hostel. Margarieta Kaiser, who owned the establishment, had a devoted love of orchids from the Machu Picchu Reserve, which surrounded the small town of Agua Caliente. As she placed her overnight bag on the cedar chest at the foot of the brass bed, Ana gazed appreciatively at the wallpaper, which had small, pale lavender orchids with yellow lips throughout it. Turning, she saw that Jake was also admiring the large, beautifully appointed room.

"See why I like to come here when I can get a day off?" she asked him wryly, coming up to him as he stood looking out the sheer white lace panel. The large rectangular window overlooked Agua Caliente's one- and two-story pastel-colored homes. Directly in front of them was the orchid-covered side of mighty Machu Picchu mountain.

Slipping her arms around his waist, Ana leaned her head against his strong back. Feeling his hands slide around her arms and cover hers, she sighed.

Jake took her full weight and absorbed Ana's warmth and nearness. She had dressed in khaki pants, hiking boots and a dark red T-shirt. To passersby, they looked like *touristas,* that was all. "Yeah, this place is nice."

"Quiet, too," Ana said. She pressed a kiss to his shoulder. Jake nodded and turned around and faced her. Just being able to look up and drown in his narrowed blue gaze was her undoing. Reaching up, Ana framed his face with her hands. Feeling the prickle of his dark beard upon her sensitive fingertips, she parted her lips and leaned upward. The softness of the *chalina* pressed against her upper body as she did so.

"I love you, Jake Travers." She brushed the hard line of his mouth with her lips. Not disappointed, she felt him smile beneath her kiss. His returning pressure upon her mouth sent scalding heat tunneling through her.

"I not only love you," Jake rasped, placing small kisses across her brow, nose and cheek, "but I want to do something about it." Easing away, he took the *chalina* from around his neck and settled it back around Ana's shoulders. He saw her smile grow deep with understanding. Eyes sparkling, she ran her fingers down the alpaca folds of the scarf.

"I accept," Ana told him, her voice choked with emotion. She held his dark, narrowed gaze. Lifting the ends of the scarf toward him, she whispered, "And I don't know how it will happen, but I want to spend my life with you, Jake. The last three months have been a great teacher to me."

Leading Ana over to the large bed, which was covered with a quilt embroidered with jungle flowers, Jake sat down next to her. "We've got a lot to talk about," he agreed quietly. Leaning down, he brought her leg up so that it rested across his thighs. As he unlaced first one boot, and then the other, he said, "I had to come back to see you, Ana. I had to know what was in your heart." He shared a brief smile with her as he set her boots next to the bed. Leaning down, he unlaced his own boots and nudged them off his feet. Turning, he settled his full length across the bed, his back resting against the decorative brass headboard. Opening his hand, he offered it to Ana.

Slipping between his thighs, Ana lay against him with her back against his chest and torso, her head resting in the juncture of his neck and shoulder. As Jake's arms came around her, his large hands splayed out across her abdomen, Ana placed her hands atop his.

"When you left," she told him softly, "my heart broke. I knew at the time you couldn't make any promises. Tal was the center of your life, not me."

Leaning down, Jake pressed a kiss to her temple, her dark hair tickling his chin. "You were, but Tal needed me more at the time." With a heavy sigh, he said, "Things really deteriorated when I got Tal home, Ana. She came apart at the seams, emotionally speaking. And on top of that, she had that bad leg that needed to heal up, too.''

Her hands tightened over his as she heard the pain and suffering in Jake's tone. ''It must have been very hard on both of you.''

''It still is,'' he told her sadly. ''Tal hasn't worked through it all. I think she's premature about coming back down here to face her ghosts from the past. She's so damn bullheaded and such a risk taker.''

Shifting her head, Ana gazed up at him. ''And you aren't a risk taker, too?'' Her mouth curved upward.

Seeing the warmth burning in her eyes, Jake shrugged. ''I guess I am. The pot calling the kettle black, maybe?''

Ana's smile widened. ''Maybe.'' She settled back against him, the smile lingering on her mouth. ''You have no idea how glad I am that you tried to write to me. When I didn't hear from you…well, I thought it was over between us….''

Jake heard the unsureness and pain in Ana's voice. ''I wrote those letters to follow the tradition of your people, Ana. Like your father wrote his letters to your mother. I don't have a doll to give you though,'' and he smiled apologetically. ''Instead, I thought I'd show up in person and plead my case with you. I guess the Peruvian post office just didn't know what to do with the address I gave them on the letters. I'm sorry I couldn't reach you, Ana. I really am. If the truth be known, I could sure have used a phone call or two from you. There were times in the last three months that I could have used your counsel—your knowing about women's things—to help me understand where Tal was at...."

Nodding, Ana pressed a small kiss to the column of his strong, thick neck. "You came back. That's all that matters. And I don't need the doll. You're right—your coming back is even better to me."

"And I brought your *chalina*."

"Yes...yes, you did." Closing her eyes, Ana whispered, "Jake, how I feel about you I've never felt about any man before. In the three months since you've left I've come to realize a lot of things. There's all kinds of love in the world, and the one I share with you is so beautiful...so rich with possibility that it scares me. I went home to my parents' the second month after you left Peru, and I sat down with them. I cried and told them all about you—and me. My mother, bless her, came over and put her arm around me after I told them everything. She told me that the way I felt about you was the way she felt about my father." Opening her eyes, Ana snagged Jake's gaze once more. "And they've been married for a very long time. They're the best of friends. They enjoy one another so much. It's wonderful to be around them. They're so inspiring to me."

"That's like my parents," Jake told her as he ran his fingers slowly up and down her arm. "They've been married for twenty-eight years. They've become dinosaurs together by today's standards, where a marriage is seen as a disposable thing you can just walk away from when the going gets tough." His mouth curved downward. His hand stilled on Ana's arm. "I'm not into disposable marriages, Ana. I know from seeing how my parents have struggled, worked, talked and made compromises with each other's needs, what marriage is really all about.''

''We both want the same thing,'' Ana agreed softly. Easing away from him, she turned, her legs tucked beneath her, framed by his large thighs. Reaching out, Ana slid her hands into his and held his stormy gaze. ''You know how dangerous my work is, Jake. And you know I'm committed to Maya, to her vision and to helping her rid Peru of the drug dealers. Every day I see our wonderful *campesinos,* entire villages, raided by drug lords and their soldiers. I want to see it stop. And I want to be a part of that process.'' Worriedly, Ana searched his darkening eyes. ''Jake, can you deal with me flying every third day and maybe dying out there in the sky over this jungle someday? I need to know that you'll support me, my vision, for my people.''

Sliding his hand over hers, Jake rasped, ''I will. I don't like it, Ana, but I accept it. I now know what a woman who's left behind when her husband goes to war feels like. The tables are turned here between us. I can't turn the love I feel for you off, and I don't want to, just because you've got a dangerous job. I know you love flying. I'd never take that away from you.''

''And what about you?'' Ana asked quietly. ''If we begin to live together, which signals a marriage among my people, what will you do?''

Taking her hand, Jake gently kissed the back of it. Her flesh was warm and slightly scented with the fragrance of what he guessed might be an orchid. Jake liked the idea that even though Ana lived and survived in a man's world, she was feminine enough to wear a fragrance. "Your captain just offered me a job," he told her wryly. "To take over supply and requisitioning for the base." He allowed a bit of a smile. "And to head up her agricultural efforts at the base. She knows I'm a farmer."

Surprised, Ana stared at him. She saw his mouth curve upward. His eyes danced with merriment. "Really? You mean, Maya would *give* you the job as our supply officer?"

"Yes. I think," Jake murmured as he trailed his fingers through her long, unbound hair, "that your C.O. knows we're in love. She's a pretty astute leader and very perceptive about people, in my opinion. She doesn't want to lose you, one of her pilots, so she was looking for a way to include me in the base ops. What do you think? She's offered us a place to stay over on the mining side of the mountain. She mentioned a little house at the bottom with some nice, fertile land just begging to be planted. My office will be located over there. All we'll have to do is live with your three-day flight schedule, and I think that will work."

Ana leaned forward, her eyes awash with tears of joy. She whispered, "I think it's wonderful." Placing a kiss on his cheek, she asked, "And will you be happy doing those jobs?"

Jake turned his head, his lips grazing hers. He felt Ana's breasts, small and firm, brush his chest as she moved into his arms. "I like a job that helps others. And getting to till the land and be a farmer again...yes, I'll be happy, Ana." His mouth closed over hers and he felt her settle into the curve of his arm as she leaned against the headboard next to him. Her mouth was soft, yielding and coaxing. Lost in her heat, the fragrant scent of orchids, Jake felt her hands moving down to divest him of his shirt. He willingly helped her.

Taking each article of clothing off one another fanned the powerful longing between them. As Ana lay down on her side again, her arms open to him, her eyes filled with desire and love, Jake knew that his life was in her hands. Her boldness, her earthy desire to come together with him upon the richly embroidered quilt decorated with flowers of the jungle that surrounded them, was in keeping with her primal essence.

Jake closed the gap between them, their naked bodies sliding beautifully together. Wrapping his leg around her more slender one, pulling her hard against him, he knew without a doubt he held heaven in his arms. Her silky hair brushed provocatively across his shoulder and down his chest as she pressed her mouth wantonly to his. Her moan galvanized him. Her hands ranging with delicious knowing across his flat, hard abdomen made him growl. He felt more animal than human as she hungrily kissed him, her moist, warm breath caressing his face.

In one movement, Jake turned onto his back and brought Ana on top of him. He watched through half-closed eyes as her thick black hair tumbled in wild abandon about her proud shoulders. As she settled across his hips, he saw her smile—the smile of a jungle cat, a feline who knew and embraced her power as a woman. Guiding her, his hands against her wide, feminine hips, he felt her sensual heat caress him. He gritted his teeth as she opened her thighs even more, her hands pressed to his chest, her fingers digging convulsively into his tightening flesh. As she eased down upon him, surrounding him in liquid heat like a tight-fitting glove, Jake felt the violent, burning knot explode within him. She moaned again, a soft, coaxing sound as she moved rhythmically against him. Like the mighty Urubamba River, which roared lustily outside their room, she was at once wild and untamed. Ana was all heat and molten lava, scalding him, burning him and freeing him with her womanly touch.

Time disintegrated for Jake. As he closed his eyes and felt Ana embracing him, nurturing him and loving him, he absorbed her every rhythmic movement into his heart. Somewhere in his spinning senses, he felt Ana tense against him. Her voice was filled with joy as she called out his name. Her fingers dug deeply into his chest. Watching the flush of pink sweep across her cheeks, her lips part and her head tilt back as she arched deeply against him, Jake felt euphoria deluge him. Gripping her hips, he guided her, thrusting deeply, again and again, into her soft, welcoming confines to prolong her pleasure. And then, without warning, the last of his massive control disintegrated and he groaned.

Ana felt his growl reverberate through her like rumbling thunder chasing a bolt of lightning. There was a roiling, writhing storm within her hotly glowing body as she moved against him to create even more pleasure for Jake. The tension in his face, the way his lips lifted away from his clenched teeth, the strength of his hands upon her hips all told her how great was his pleasure as his life flowed into her welcoming body.

Ana whispered his name like a fervent prayer and fell across him, her legs tangling with his in the aftermath. They lay in one another's arms, their bodies slick and heated. Nuzzling his jaw, she placed tiny kisses along it and closed her eyes, exhausted. Just the way Jake weakly caressed her back made her smile. The bed was soft and comfortable. Jake was hard and male, and Ana reveled in their differences. Together, they made a complete whole.

Breathing raggedly, Ana whispered, "You are *Inti,* the sun, and I am *K'uychi,* your rainbow."

She felt so giving and sustaining within Jake's arms. Easing onto his side and bringing Ana against him, he rose up on his elbow, her black hair a coverlet across it. Caressing her damp cheek, he rasped, "I like how you see us. And I like the world you live in, Ana. It's close to nature, like us."

She gazed tenderly into his stormy blue eyes. "We are a part of nature. Wild and free—" she ran her fingers across his unmarred brow "—like Father Sun and Mother Moon."

"I like you being my rainbow, because you really are, you know…." And Jake leaned down and kissed her soft, parted lips, once more drinking Ana into his heart and soul.

Jake awoke slowly. He had no idea what time it was. In addition to the exhausting flight, the tension and worry about Ana and how she would respond to him had taken a massive emotional toll on him. He lay on his back with Ana snuggled against his length. Turning his head, he saw there was no longer any light coming through the panels at the window. Lifting his wrist, he looked at his watch. It was 9:00 p.m.

Ana stirred in his arms, made a small sound resembling a moan and began to stretch her full length like an awakening jaguar.

Jake wondered if he'd woken her. They lay with the thick quilt across them. "Go back to sleep," he rasped.

"Mmm...what time is it?"

"Twenty-one hundred hours," he said, dropping into military time for her. She felt so warm and alive in his arms. Jake luxuriated in the feel of her strong body against his. There wasn't an ounce of fat on Ana, and he realized the stress and strain of her job as an assault gunship pilot had a lot to do with that. Maybe, with them living together, he could add a good ten pounds to her frame. She needed it, he realized, as he ran his fingers down her rib cage and settled his hand on her hip.

"I'm hungry...." Ana whispered wickedly, and she opened her eyes to meet his gaze. As she sat up, her eyes glimmered. Jake was grinning at her, his face deeply shadowed. He hadn't shaved and now his beard made him look even more dangerous and alluring. "Well..." she said drowsily, "let me amend that—I'm hungry for you and for some food."

"So am I."

Laughing softly, Ana tilted her head, leaned down and kissed him lingeringly upon his smiling mouth. "Which one first?" she asked against his lips. Absorbing his tender touch as he ran his hand across her back and down her arm, Ana drowned in his lambent gaze. This was how she wanted to awaken every morning for the rest of her life—with Jake.

"Well," he murmured, giving her a slight poke in the ribs, "you are way too skinny, sweetheart. I think a big Peruvian meal of pink trout is what you need first."

"And dessert?"

He met her merry look. "You're my dessert."

With a lilting laugh, Ana sat up and stretched languidly. "You always say the right thing to make me feel happy!"

Jake slowly sat up in turn, the quilt falling away from him. "No," he told her wryly, "I'm sure there's going to be plenty of times when I put my foot in my mouth with you." He reached out and slid a strand of her silky hair between his thumb and index finger. Ana's face grew sultry with invitation. Already his body was responding once more to that smoldering look in her large cinnamon eyes. "I can only hope you'll sit down with me and we'll talk it out. If we talk, we'll avoid a lot of problems."

Ana caught his hand and kissed each of his fingertips. "We'll talk—a lot. I promise." Releasing Jake's hand, she poked his ribs. "You're skinny, too, you know. You've lost weight, Jake."

Nodding, he said, "The last three months have been hell on me emotionally, Ana. I didn't have much of an appetite.'' He eased off the bed and went to the bathroom where he turned on the taps of the huge bathtub on brass claw feet. When he returned, he enjoyed watching Ana slip off the bed and walk toward him. There was such sureness and confidence in her step, in the way she moved and carried herself. She was proud, beautiful and courageous.

''Let's bathe one another,'' she said, ''and then let's go down to India Feliz Restaurant. Patrick's staff catches the trout right out of the Urubamba River on the other side of town.''

Jake liked the idea of sliding into a tub of hot water with Ana. As she moved past him, she lifted her hair off her shoulders and quickly wound it into a thick braid atop her head. Her every movement was like a small miracle to him. She was graceful, her fingers slender and feminine. Fingers that had loved him, had made his body harden and sing, just hours before.

His stomach growled. Ana looked over at him. ''I think we need to feed you.''

Later, as they lingered over mocha lattes at a table on the second floor of the India Feliz, Jake blocked out the murmurs of the many patrons who now filled Patrick's very popular establishment. After consuming a huge meal of *trucha,* trout, served with the most delicious potatoes he'd ever eaten, he felt completely sated. Across from him, Ana's soft smile made his heart throb with desire for her all over again. She sat with her elbows on the pale pink linen tablecloth, a delicate china cup decorated with flowers in her hands. The look on her features told Jake everything.

For the first time, he was seeing Ana truly relaxed. She'd eaten almost half of her dinner, far more than she would have ordinarily, she told him. Jake was sure her appetite was because of their enthusiastic lovemaking earlier.

"You know what I'd like to do tomorrow morning?" Ana asked, a wistful note in her voice.

"Name it," Jake said. He picked up his cup and finished off the rich chocolate drink.

"Let's take the civilian helicopter to Rainbow Valley," Ana murmured in a low tone, because she didn't want patrons who sat nearby to overhear them. She saw the surprise and then the question in Jake's eyes. Setting the cup down, she said, "I want you to meet my parents, Jake. In the tradition of my people, I must present you to them. If you'll wear my *chalina* tomorrow, they'll know." Her smile increased. "I know my parents will approve of you...of us. They know all about you, so I'm sure they'll be happy to finally meet you."

Nodding, Jake said, "That's fine. I'd like to meet the two people who made such a beautiful daughter." He reached out and slid his hand into hers.

Ana's eyes glistened with love for him. "I know my parents will want to hold a feast in our honor, later. All my relations will be invited." Her voice became filled with excitement. "You'll get to meet my mother's side of the family, the *campesino* side, and all my father's relations from Cusco and Lima. It will be a wonderful all-day, and all-night celebration. We'll dance. We'll sing. We'll laugh. We'll cry.

It will be a time you'll never forget.'' She smiled longingly into his eyes.

Giving her hand a squeeze, Jake asked, ''And can I invite my parents down here? And ask Tal to attend?''

She smiled. ''Of course! It is tradition that both sets of parents of a couple meet and approve of their relationship.''

''Good.'' The joy in Ana's eyes matched how Jake felt in his heart. ''I think Tal will be happy for us. She kept needling me while I was home with her in Iowa, about you—us—and how I felt about you.''

''She knew,'' Ana said quietly. ''As much as she was suffering, Tal could see your love for me.''

Mouth quirking, Jake tightened his fingers around Ana's momentarily. ''Yes, and she saw your love for me, as well. Tal isn't dumb by a long shot. Maybe…well, maybe this coming celebration will help her heal. I hope it does.''

''People in love always spread their joy to those around them,'' Ana said simply. ''Perhaps it will start a healing process within Tal. We can only hope.''

Patrick, dressed in white pants, white apron and shirt as befitting his rank as a French chef, came over to them. In his hand, he held out a delicious-looking dessert of strawberries and whipping cream with thick yellow Bavarian pudding surrounding it, sprinkled with slivers of almond. On top was a small puff pastry decorated in pink and white icing resembling tiny flowers.

''For you, *mon chérie*,'' he told Ana in broken English. ''And for your young man here. To celebrate.''

Patrick smiled, his narrow face and dark eyes sparkling as he straightened after setting the dessert between them. He pointed to the *chalina* that Jake wore around his neck. "I see you have chosen, Ana. Congratulations to you both." And he held out his slender hand to Jake.

Jake shook his hand and thanked him. He didn't know French, but wished he did now as Patrick, who was in his early forties, his black hair short and shining beneath the lamps above, tried his best to convey his heartfelt sentiments in English.

Ana was thrilled. "*Merci,* Patrick. This is a wonderful celebration gift!"

Patrick stood there, his hands on his hips, his face filled with pride. "*Oui, mon chérie.* I know how you love my desserts. When I saw this *norteamericano* come in wearing your *chalina,* I knew." His mouth curved faintly. "I knew you had chosen. We must celebrate your coming together, eh? Soon? Perhaps Maya will attend? *Oui?*"

"*Oui,*" Ana said, touched. Reaching out, she squeezed Patrick's arm. "You are so wonderful to all of us. We're so lucky to have you here in Agua Caliente." Sharing a warm look with Jake, Ana added, "And yes, let's plan a wonderful celebration for Jake and me. Probably half the people I know will come." Ana knew that Patrick was aware of their secret base, but he never said anything to anyone about it. He'd been living in Agua Caliente for years, knew the lay of the land and had opened his establishment as a home away from home to those who lived at the base.

Patrick bowed deeply. "It will be my honor, Ana."

As he straightened he pointed energetically at the dessert. "I would suggest you open the puff pastry."

Ana gave him a quizzical look, her fork suspended over the dessert. "Oh?"

"Oui," Patrick said sagely, his black eyebrows arching with authority. "Please, open it—carefully, however…"

Puzzled, Ana gave Jake a quizzical look, shrugged and, with her fingers and the help of the fork, pried open the four-cornered puff pastry. Then she gasped.

"Jake!"

Patrick chuckled and slapped his thigh.

Ana's eyes grew huge as she saw the gold ring with a single diamond solitaire sitting in the middle of the pastry on a small satin cushion. Her gaze shot across the table. Jake was grinning up at Patrick, and they were congratulating one another heartily.

"Oh…" Ana whispered, in shock as she carefully removed the ring from the pink satin cushion. As she held it up to the light, the diamond solitaire sparkled with fire in its depths. Tears jammed her eyes as she looked up at Jake, who was smiling tenderly at her, hope burning in his eyes.

"Do you like it?" he asked, his voice off-key with emotion.

Patrick clapped his hands. "Of course she likes it! What woman would not like such a gift?" He leaned over and kissed each of Ana's cheeks, then he shook Jake's hand once more. "A very good plan you had," he exclaimed enthusiastically. Then he gestured discreetly to one of his waiters, a young Que'ro who hurried over with a bottle of champagne in a bucket and two champagne glasses.

"To celebrate your good fortune," Patrick told them. "The meal, everything, is on the house tonight, for both of you. Enjoy!" And he left, smiling grandly.

In shock, Ana barely could speak as the waiter, Isidro, carefully popped the champagne cork and slowly poured the golden, bubbly liquid into the glasses. Smiling shyly at them, he bowed slightly and left them alone.

"Oh, Jake…" Ana whispered. "I—I'm in shock! I never expected…"

Grinning from ear to ear, Jake took the ring from her and picked up her left hand. "Let's see if it fits?" His heart beat hard in his chest. Ana's cheeks were pink, her eyes sparkling with tears and her beautiful mouth parted breathlessly with happiness.

Holding her left hand across the table, Jake eased the ring onto it. The diamond glinted like a fiery rainbow as she raised it and showed it off to him. "It fits perfectly, Jake."

Catching her hand, he pressed a warm kiss to the back of it. "Do you like it?"

"Like it? I love it!" Ana caressed the stone, her lower lip trembling.

Her reaction made Jake feel so good. Handing her one glass, he said, "Let's drink to our lives—together, Ana."

Touched, Ana nodded. The glasses clinked pleasantly together and she drank a small amount of the bubbly liquid. The look in Jake's eyes told her everything. Her hand tingled where the ring touched it. She was stunned by his planning.

"Patrick must have loved your romantic idea," she said accusingly as she set the champagne glass down on the table.

Giving her a proud look, Jake said, "Yeah, he liked the idea, although I had a helluva time trying to explain it to him, not knowing any French. And he doesn't know much English. I drew a lot of sketches for him and he got it," Jake chuckled.

Laughing, Ana nodded. "Patrick knows French, Spanish and Quechua. English is a distant—very distant—fourth language for him, and he really struggles with it. Bless his heart, though. Look what he did for us." Ana gazed at Jake and saw the joy in his eyes. "You're such a wonderful person, Jake." Reaching across the table, she whispered, "And I love you so much...."

As their fingers touched and Jake grasped her slender hand with his, he vowed huskily, "And I'll love you forever, Ana. Forever..."

*　*　*　*　*

ATTENTION LINDSAY McKENNA FANS!
Maya's story will be available
next month!

Look for

MORGAN'S MERCENARIES:
HEART OF STONE

a longer-length, single title
on sale in March 2001 at
your favorite retail outlets!

Turn the page for a sneak preview....

Chapter One

He wanted to see her. As repelled as he was by the assignment, there was something in him that ached to see Maya once again. That surprised Dane more than anything else. How could he miss someone who had been such a thorn in his side? Challenging him? Confronting him daily as she'd done at school all those years ago?

The crews hurriedly took the two Apaches he and his crew had flown in and moved them farther into the cave where they couldn't be seen. As the helicopters slowly rolled by, Dane saw four women pilots, helmets tucked beneath their arms, standing in a circle and talking animatedly to one another. It was easy to pick out Maya. She stood above all of them like the Amazon warrior she was.

The drift of the women's laughter made him tense. And then, he saw Maya lift her head and look directly at him. He felt a heated prickle at the base of his neck—a warning—as her eyes settled flatly on him. At this distance, he couldn't make out her expression. He could, however, feel the coming confrontation.

Mouth going dry, Dane watched as she walked toward him, her chin up, her black flowing hair moving across her proud shoulders. The other three pilots, as if in formation, walked on either side of her. They looked like proud, confident, fierce warriors even though they were women. As they passed through the bright shafts of sunlight now shining strongly through the eye of the cave, he watched the golden radiance embrace them.

Locking on to Maya's assessing emerald green gaze, he rocked internally from the power of her formidable presence. She was even more stunning looking than he could recall. In the four years since he'd been her instructor pilot, she had grown and matured. Her black hair shone with reddish tones as the sunlight embraced her stalwart form. Her skin was a golden color, cheekbones high, that set of glorious green eyes framed by thick, black arching brows. But it was the play of a half smile, one corner of her full lips cocked upward, and that slightly dimpled chin and clean jawline, that made him feel momentarily shaky.

She could have been a model strutting down a Paris runway instead of the proficient Apache helicopter pilot she was. The snug-fitting one-piece black flight suit she wore carved out every inch of her statuesque form. She was big boned, and had a lot of firm muscle beneath that material, but there wasn't an ounce of fat anywhere on her that he could see. She was all legs, her hips wide to reflect the fact that she was woman, and she was slightly short-waisted. All thoroughbred. All woman.

A powerful, confident woman.

Dane saw laughter in her large green eyes. He felt his palms grow sweaty and his heart raced as she closed the gap between them. They were like two consummate warriors, wary and distrustful, circling one another to try and see where the chinks in each other's armor were, where the Achilles' heel was, so that one of them might get the upper hand first, and be victorious.

And when he felt the shaft of desire that shot through him as she stood before him, her green eyes still locked with his, he wasn't so sure who would be the victor this time....

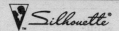

Silhouette

SPECIAL EDITION™

is delighted to present

The **Stockwells** *of Texas*

Available January—May 2001

**Where family secrets, scandalous pasts
and unexpected love wreak havoc on the lives
of the infamous Stockwells of Texas!**

THE TYCOON'S INSTANT DAUGHTER
by Christine Rimmer
(SE #1369) on sale January 2001

SEVEN MONTHS AND COUNTING...
by Myrna Temte
(SE #1375) on sale February 2001

HER UNFORGETTABLE FIANCÉ
by Allison Leigh
(SE #1381) on sale March 2001

THE MILLIONAIRE AND THE MOM
by Patricia Kay
(SE #1387) on sale April 2001

THE CATTLEMAN AND THE VIRGIN HEIRESS
by Jackie Merritt
(SE #1393) on sale May 2001

Available at your favorite retail outlet.

Silhouette®

Where love comes alive™

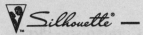

where love comes alive—online...

eHARLEQUIN.com

shop eHarlequin

- ♥ Find all the new Silhouette releases at everyday great discounts.
- ♥ Try before you buy! Read an excerpt from the latest Silhouette novels.
- ♥ Write an online review and share your thoughts with others.

reading room

- ♥ Read our Internet exclusive daily and weekly online serials, or vote in our interactive novel.
- ♥ Talk to other readers about your favorite novels in our Reading Groups.
- ♥ Take our Choose-a-Book quiz to find the series that matches you!

authors' alcove

- ♥ Find out interesting tidbits and details about your favorite authors' lives, interests and writing habits.
- ♥ Ever dreamed of being an author? Enter our Writing Round Robin. The Winning Chapter will be published online! Or review our writing guidelines for submitting your novel.

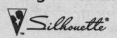

Don't miss the reprisal of
Silhouette Romance's popular miniseries

When King Michael of Edenbourg goes missing,

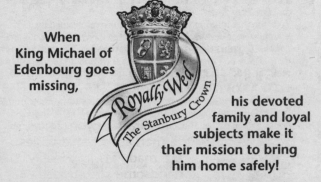

his devoted family and loyal subjects make it their mission to bring him home safely!

Their search begins March 2001 and continues through June 2001.

On sale March 2001: **THE EXPECTANT PRINCESS**
by bestselling author **Stella Bagwell** (SR #1504)

On sale April 2001: **THE BLACKSHEEP PRINCE'S BRIDE**
by rising star **Martha Shields** (SR #1510)

On sale May 2001: **CODE NAME: PRINCE**
by popular author **Valerie Parv** (SR #1516)

On sale June 2001: **AN OFFICER AND A PRINCESS**
by award-winning author **Carla Cassidy** (SR #1522)

Available at your favorite retail outlet.

Where love comes alive™

COMING NEXT MONTH

#1381 HER UNFORGETTABLE FIANCÉ—Allison Leigh
Stockwells of Texas
To locate her missing mother, Kate Stockwell teamed up
with private investigator Brett Larson to masquerade as a married
couple. Together they discovered that desire still burned between
them. But when former fiancé Brett asked Kate to be his wife for
real, she feared that she could never provide all that he wanted...

#1382 A LOVE BEYOND WORDS—Sherryl Woods
Firefighter Enrique Wilder saved Allie Matthews from the rubble
of her home and forever changed her silent world. A shared
house and an undeniable chemistry caused passion to run high.
But would Allie be able to love a man who lived so close to
danger?

#1383 WIFE IN DISGUISE—Susan Mallery
Lone Star Canyon
Josie Scott decided it was time to resolve the past and showed
up at her ex-husband's door a changed woman. Friendship and
closure were all that Josie was after, until she looked into
Del Scott's eyes. Finally, with a chance to explore their
daunting past, would the two discover that love was still alive?

#1384 STANDING BEAR'S SURRENDER—Peggy Webb
Forlorn former Blue Angel pilot Jim Standing Bear had lost his
ambition...until he found gentle beauty Sarah Sloan. She
reminded Jim that he was all man. But Sarah—committed to
caring for another—would have to choose between loyalty and
true love....

#1385 SEPARATE BEDROOMS...?—Carole Halston
All Cara LaCroix wanted was to fulfill her grandmother's final
wish—to see her granddaughter marry a good man. So when
childhood friend Neil Griffen offered his help, Cara accepted.
Could their brief marriage of convenience turn into an everlasting
covenant of love?

#1386 HOME AT LAST—Laurie Campbell
Desperate for a detective's help, Kirsten Laurence called old
flame J. D. Ryder. She didn't have romance on her mind, but they
soon found themselves in each other's arms. Would their embrace
withstand the shocking revelation of Kirsten's long-kept secret?